Mr. Pleasant

Mr.
Pleasant

Jim Ray Daniels

Michigan State University Press • *East Lansing*

♾ The paper used in this publication meets the minimum requirements
of ANSI/NISO Z39.48-1992 (R 1997) (Permanence of Paper).

Michigan State University Press
East Lansing, Michigan 48823-5245

Printed and bound in the United States of America.

13 12 11 10 09 08 07   1 2 3 4 5 6 7 8 9 10

LIBRARY OF CONGRESS CATALOGING-IN-PUBLICATION DATA
Daniels, Jim Ray.
Mr. Pleasant / Jim Ray Daniels.
p. cm.
ISBN 978-0-87013-806-5 (pbk. : alk. paper)
I. Title.
PS3604.A5335M7 2007
813'.6–dc22
2007025089

ACKNOWLEDGMENTS
Great River Review: "No Man's Land"
Night Train: "United States Street Football"
Paper Train: "Society of Friends"
Ward 3: "Closing Costs"

Cover design by Erin Kirk New
Book design/layout by Sharp Des!gns, Inc.
Cover photograph: "Untitled, Pittsburgh, PA c. 1985," by Charlee Brodsky.
Used by permission of the photographer.

Michigan State University Press is a member of the Green Press Initiative and is
committed to developing and encouraging ecologically responsible publishing practices.
For more information about the Green Press Initiative and the use of recycled paper in
book publishing, please visit www.greenpressinitiative.org.

■

Visit Michigan State University Press on the World Wide Web at **www.msupress.msu.edu**

Contents

Mr. Pleasant

The Human Error

When Carol's daughter's suitcase blew off the car-top carrier, I should have known we were in trouble. Rhonda was twelve, and losing that suitcase of hers along the Ohio Turnpike was about the worst thing I could've done. She'd been listening to old tapes from my band days—I've got boxes of our cassettes and CDs in my closet—and I'd been beginning to think I had a chance with her.

"Damn it, Frank, we've got to find that suitcase," Carol hissed under her breath, though Rhonda could hear her. It was Christmas, and I was taking them to Detroit to meet my parents. We'd stopped at a rest area and noticed it missing when we got out of the car. The other suitcases were still there, bungeed up tight. If she hadn't made me pull hers off at the last minute to add some mysterious paper bag, this would have never happened. I'd wedged it back in under just one of the bungees before hitting the road. She'd messed with my beautiful bungee grid system. I would've had to redo the whole thing to get it back in securely.

"What was in that bag?" I asked.

Rhonda glared at me. "It doesn't matter now, does it?"

"Why does everybody think this was my fault?" I kicked off the chunk of dirty snow packed behind the wheel well.

"Now I gotta meet those people with no clothes. They're gonna think I'm a freak."

"Stop calling them *those people*—they're my parents."

"We'll buy you some new things in Detroit," Carol said.

I hoped Carol didn't mean using my credit card—it was already maxed out by Christmas. We'd come 173 miles already, according to my odometer. I knew it was exactly 301 miles from Pittsburgh to my parents' door in Detroit. I was twenty-nine years old, and I wanted to marry Carol. I'd explained that I wasn't taking her home for their approval—it was simply to have them at least meet her before we ran off and got married. I had a job repairing copying machines, and it paid pretty well. I'd stopped playing in bands two years earlier—I just couldn't handle the late-night gigs anymore, not for what we were getting paid. I was finishing up my associate's degree in information systems at CCAC. An almost degree at an almost college, my father called it, though he didn't know college from roadkill.

I was turning into roadkill myself in that stiff turnpike wind. In Ohio, nothing stops the wind—it roars across the flat land and smacks the hell out of whatever's in its way. Twenty miles to the next exit, which meant we'd have to drive forty miles just to begin retracing our steps, since U-turns on the turnpike were illegal. I'd jumped bail on a drunk driving charge in a small town in Ohio six years ago, and with computers and everything, they probably had me listed somewhere.

I sighed, the cloud of my breath quickly disintegrating in the breeze. I wanted a cigarette in the worst way—just that little red heat to suck in. I'd only quit six months ago. For Carol, I quit. "Honey, we can't go back," I said. "It could be anywhere. It could've happened when I pulled out of the driveway, for chrissake."

Rhonda had this look on her face in the backseat. I could read her lips. She was motherfucking me to her little brother, Danny.

"Should she be talking that way in front of Danny?" He was six.

"Why can't we go back?"

"Or some car smashed it to smithereens. My parents are waiting on us for dinner."

Carol got back in the car, slamming the door, then opening it and slamming it again just to be sure I understood.

■ ■ ■

My mother's present for me was a clock that makes different bird-calls every hour. She got it from Lillian Vernon. If it's not in that catalogue, then she's not buying. She does all her Christmas shopping with one phone call, sitting at the kitchen table next to her walker. I keep telling her she doesn't have to get me anything, but she always says, "If I can't do this, I may as well die." My parents wanted me to move back to Detroit. My sister was stuck taking care of them both, and that wasn't fair. I drove home a lot on weekends, across the Ohio Turnpike—by myself, until now.

I put the batteries in the clock, and it immediately played all twelve birdcalls.

"Now, ain't that something?" I said, bending over to give my mom a big smacky kiss.

"Frankie always loved the birds. Let me show you the birdhouse he made for me when he was in Scouts," she said to Carol. She never threw anything away that I'd made or given her. She had a system to keep track of everything. The whole house was one big system. The wall unit now was filled with nativity sets from around the world. In the spring, it'd be the birdhouses, including the mis-shapen one I wove for her when Mrs. Nella was my den mother. The Nellas hated me still because I kicked Oscar out of the Human

Error years ago for smoking too much wacky tobacky and forgetting the words to the songs.

"Don't worry about that now. Why don't you open *your* present? It's from me and Carol—and the kids."

Danny, crouched beneath the Christmas tree, was playing with the nativity figures. Carol hadn't taken her kids to church since she got kicked out for getting divorced. I was hoping he wouldn't do anything weird with baby Jesus. That'd set my parents off. They were old-school Catholics.

She fumbled with the ribbons, and her stiff fingers struggled with the paper till she finally reached the box, opened it, and stared, speechless.

"It's a plastic-bag drier," I said quickly. "I saw you washing them out and drying them in the dish drainer. This'll dry them real fast." My mother reused everything. In fact, at that moment, she was carefully folding up the wrapping paper.

"How thoughtful," she said. "Where'd you find such a thing?"

"Kaufmann's," I said. Kaufmann's was a large department store in Pittsburgh. I'd been proud of myself—the bag drier was a real Lillian Vernon kind of gift. It didn't cost much, but with my mother, that made it more valuable. If you spent a lot of money on something for her, she'd frown and demand that you take it back. I'd tried to explain that to Carol, who'd wanted to get her a nice dress.

"Well, I'm going to have to tell Lillian about these." She seemed disappointed, as if Lillian Vernon had let her down for missing out on such an essential item.

"Carol picked it out," I lied.

"Oh, thank you, dear," my mother said. "Do you shop with Lillian Vernon? They have so many wonderful things!"

My mother had picked out Christmas tea towels for Carol that said "Christmas Carol" on them.

My parents named me after Saint Francis of Assisi. I've been

4

reading up on him lately, trying to figure out the Big Deal and where I fit in. I've decided that he was the *true* son of God. I don't have proof, but my hunches are usually pretty accurate. I'd like to go to Italy someday to check it out. This big earthquake trashed his church back in Assisi a couple of years ago, and that was obviously some kind of sign. Now, this isn't something I talk about with a lot of people. If I'm wrong, I'm rotting in hell big-time. If there is a hell.

I bent down and pulled Danny away from the nativity figures, whispering, "Those aren't toys, buddy." The divorce had not seemed to affect Danny much, since he was only four at the time, but who knew what was going on in his little head.

"Which one's the daddy?" he said loudly, refusing to let go of the shepherd with the lamb around his neck.

I looked up to Carol for help, but it was too late. My father got down on the floor and started in explaining all the figures, as if he'd been waiting precisely for that moment.

"This is Joseph, now he's kind of the daddy, but not really. You know about Joseph, right?" Danny stared up at him blankly, clutching the shepherd in his fist. My father glared over at us on the couch, then turned back to Danny.

"Of course, the real daddy is God. God the Father. And this baby, this is God, too. The Son of God—Jesus Christ, the Lord our Savior."

"Two daddies. I got two daddies," Danny said.

"Frank ain't your daddy," Rhonda mumbled sullenly from the floor next to the TV. "Can we turn this on?"

"Sure, let's turn it on," my mother said, quickly hitting the remote. They didn't have cable, so the options were limited. She found "Mr. Magoo's Christmas Carol." It was something Danny had seen at home, and he moved away from the nativity set and onto the rug in the middle of the floor to watch. He was still clutching the shepherd—I had to pry it from his hands while he slept later that night. Rhonda quickly got bored and went into the room she was sharing with Carol. I was sharing one with Danny. My parents didn't want us sleeping together "under their roof," and Rhonda refused to share a room with Danny, anyway.

■ ■ ■

Carol's parents were both long dead—cancer and cancer. Somebody was doing a study of the high cancer rate in her old neighborhood. It was downstream from a chemical plant that dumped all kinds of shit into the water. They called it "Orange Creek" when she was growing up, because the water was literally orange. Her father had worked at that plant. I think losing both her parents early on did funny things to Carol's head. She seemed all messed up about visiting my parents—half sad, half jealous.

"Your dad sounds like an asshole," she'd said the night before we left.

"I just want to prepare you. He's not what you call a sensitive guy."

"Oh, and you are?" she said, and gave her quick, nervous, high-pitched laugh, the one that threatened to spiral out of control into madness when she was scared or felt threatened.

"You mean, he's the strong, silent type?" she said.

"Nah. He's not strong or silent," I said. "He's weak and loud." I regretted putting down my father like that, but it was how I felt. He made up for his weakness by being loud. He was half-deaf from working at the GM axle plant down the road, and that job made him so powerless he often took it out on us at home. I knew I never wanted to work in a plant like my father—and like half the kids in my high school. And I knew I wanted to leave Detroit.

"And my mom's sweet and crazy," I said. "Sweet with pepper in it. Crazy like an ox."

"You mean fox?"

"No, ox. It's her defense mechanism. She's stubbornly crazy."

■ ■ ■

My mother had insisted on preparing a huge, traditional Christmas dinner—turkey, stuffing, the works. She'd never been what you'd call a great cook, but she was consistent, reliable. She had her small repertoire, and she stuck with it. Turkey had been one thing she knew how to cook, though both she and my father had developed an extreme fear of undercooked meat, so she'd taken to cooking everything dry. That poor bird never had a chance.

The kids filled their plates. We'd stopped for lunch at a new rest stop in the no-man's-land between Cleveland and Toledo, but when the suitcase was gone, so were our appetites. They were expecting the delicious, home-cooked, grandmotherly meal they'd seen on made-for-TV movies. The turkey meat looked like shredded newspaper, and my baked potato dropped like a stone onto my plate.

Carol wanted to sit next to Danny, but my dad insisted she sit between him and my mother. "Let's pray," my father said.

"Okay," said Danny. "I never prayed before."

"Well, you're gonna learn," my father said. He recited the blessing, by the book. He never varied from the script, even on holidays. Danny tried to imitate the sign of the cross—it looked like he was doing some sleight-of-hand trick. Rhonda just shrugged and held her hands in her lap.

"Now put your napkins in your laps," my father said.

"Dad, chill out," I said. "Carol's their mom."

"Hmmph," my father said.

The kids quickly dug into their meals, then quickly stopped.

Danny gagged and spit up the stuffing onto his plate.

Rhonda had been trying to slice her potato when it skidded off her plate onto the floor. Danny laughed. I saw tears streaking Carol's cheek as she bent to her plate, silently chewing and chewing at the tough meat like it was old gum.

"Great dinner," my father said. "Right, everyone?"

"Right. Great dinner, Mom," I said. None of the Crystals said a word. And it was clear that they were the Crystals, and we were the Mullinses, and that at that moment, we did not belong at the same table, or in the same universe.

"Better clean your plates, kids, if you want some of those great pies out in the kitchen," my father said.

"Fat chance," Rhonda grumbled.

"Leave the table. Now," Carol said, and she did. Then Carol got up and followed her. "Excuse me," she said.

"The pies are good. I checked," I said. And I had—snuck a little sliver of pumpkin. They were fine. If we just could've had the pies and dispensed with everything else, maybe things would have worked out better.

I surreptitiously scraped Danny's plate onto Rhonda's so his looked clean. Nobody said another word, but we got our pie, and ate seconds, with whipped cream.

My mother wiped Danny's mouth with a wet cloth. I think my parents had been looking forward to having kids around again. Maybe since I'd turned out so lousy, they wanted another crack at it.

My older sister, Betty, was gay, though the reality of that had never penetrated my parents' minds. At least, they'd never let on that it had. Even when Betty bought a house with her partner, Anne. My mother called them "the girls." Betty had never told them explicitly, though she never tried to hide anything. They liked Anne—more than they liked me, it seemed. They must've known there weren't any kids coming out of that side of the family, though my mother occasionally suggested to me that Betty "might still meet some nice man one of these days."

Betty and Anne were away at Anne's sister's in Chicago. I could've used them both in Detroit with us. I suppose to some it might seem sad that we needed two lesbians to give our Christmas some semblance of normalcy, but we were all used to having them there for the holidays, and they could've given everyone a comfort zone—particularly Carol and her kids. In that tiny house it seemed like you couldn't take a step without brushing against the prickly needles of the Christmas tree.

■　■　■

I hadn't picked up a guitar in almost a year, though I used to think I couldn't live without it. My parents were thrilled when I gave up the band and started settling down, so they had a vested interest in liking Carol, despite her being divorced and an "older woman"—she was thirty-four. She seemed ordinary enough, even to me. No tattoos or multicolored hair, no revealing outfits or lingering drug habits. Carol worked as a secretary in the Slavic Languages department at the University of Pittsburgh. Her father was an immigrant from Serbia, and she occasionally did translation work on the side.

I ended up in Pittsburgh because of the band. They loved us in Pittsburgh, I don't know why. They kept asking us back to play till we got offered a weekly gig at Graffiti, one of the best clubs in town—a deal we'd never get back in Detroit, where everyone knew us as just another local cover band, despite the fact that we'd been writing our own songs for years. It was hard to change our early reputation, so we just packed up and moved. Within a year, we broke up, and the others all went back to Detroit. Pittsburgh isn't a big stretch from Detroit, but it's different enough for people back home to say, "Pittsburgh, why'd you stay in Pittsburgh?" And I could simply say, "They liked me there."

I used to be the best dancer in the band, no matter who else was in it. I always got my moments strutting at the front of the stage with my guitar. My nickname was Feet, though more than one embittered former bandmate said that the trouble was I played guitar with my feet, too. I'm experienced with breakups—I was in eight bands in thirteen years. Of course, some of them overlapped personnel. In one band, we kept losing singers. The rest of us weren't quite so interested in the singer being "The Man" in the band. The Straight Jackets, the Mumps, the Measles, the Blue Streaks, Muffin, the Human Error, the Plastic Monsters, and, my favorite, the Frank Mullins Band. Of course, that's me.

Carol met me at a gig. She was out with some friends, one of whom, Jaquinta, was a regular at our shows. It was clear Carol didn't get out much because of her kids—she was way overdressed—a white, clingy dress with flowers. Something you might wear to a wedding shower but not to a Plastic Monsters show. Jaquinta introduced me to Carol while the band was on break, and I asked her out before we started our next set. My girlfriend Jill had dumped me two weeks earlier. I was in a hurry to make a new start. Within a month, I'd formed Muffin with Roger, the bass player, and I was sleeping at Carol's on weekends.

Our first date was dinner at her house. I know people say that's all wrong, meeting her kids on the first date, but Carol was no-nonsense. If her kids didn't like me, she wasn't going to waste her time. She put me to the test with her kids, just like I was putting her to the test with my parents. Rhonda and Danny were stiffly polite as we sat at the table chewing takeout chicken. They liked extra crispy, so we spent a lot of time crunching at each other while Carol fussed around with the bags and plates as if she'd cooked it herself. And I kept saying, "Great chicken, Carol." I couldn't help myself.

"Yeah, great chicken," Rhonda said in her perpetually sarcastic voice, though I did get a small smile out of her with my nervous repetitions. Sweet Danny just shouted, "Great chicken, Mom!" with intense sincerity. I took them to Dairy Queen for ice cream and passed with a C.

Carol looked much younger than she was. Great figure, long black hair. Tall. Big green eyes, as if she were perpetually excited or surprised. Her ex-husband, Jerry, sold cars at McKeon Buick and was taking Latin dance classes with his new girlfriend, Bee, Carol's ex-best friend. I met Bee once, and she didn't look nearly as good as Carol. Maybe Jerry knew something I didn't, or maybe he was just a loser, like everyone else I ever knew who sold cars for a living.

■　■　■

"Oh, Terry Reid wants you to call him. I told his mother you were coming to town," my mother said while we squirmed in silence in the crowded living room after dinner. Carol and Rhonda had finally emerged. It looked like they'd both been crying. They sat together on the couch, holding hands.

Terry had been the bass player in at least three of my bands. He'd stayed in Pittsburgh the longest, though now was back home, married to Betty Moreno, his high school sweetheart. They'd gotten together again at a reunion. It was "such a sweet story," my mother had said one time too many, thinking, perhaps, of the lack of sweet stories in my own life.

I hadn't seen Terry since his wedding. "When did he call?"

"Oh, last week sometime. His number's somewhere by the phone."

■　■　■

"Didn't your mom tell you?" Terry asked after we'd dispensed with the ho-ho-ho holiday greetings. "We're having a band reunion. Everybody's in town. It's tonight, dude. At Saint Margaret's, just like the old days."

"Which band?"

"Hell, I don't know—all of 'em. Maybe half Mumps, half Plastic Monsters. Hey, bring your new old lady."

"She's got kids."

"Bring the kids. I'm bringing mine."

"I'm rusty. All I can play these days is the copying machine."

"You think we're not? No audience—it's family. A family reunion. For fun."

"I can't remember, was it fun?"

"Asshole. You know it was fun. For a long time, anyway."

"Yeah, damn it, it *was* a hell of a lot of fun." My parents had never gotten a portable phone, or a cell phone, or an answering machine. I was stuck to the kitchen wall, listening to everyone else listening. Just like in the old days. "Tonight?"

"Yeah, eight o'clock—we've all got to get to bed a lot earlier these days, eh, bro?"

"That's the truth." Suddenly my whole life at that moment seemed to consist of bodies of pressure pushing in on me. I closed my eyes and tried to imagine the mad, spontaneous feedback of those bands. "I'll be there."

■ ■ ■

"Be where?" my mother asked.

"Yeah," Carol said. "Where?"

"Mom, Terry told you all about it. A band reunion—why didn't you tell me?"

"I didn't think you'd have time with you leaving tomorrow."

"Thought you'd just want to spend time here at home," my father weighed in. "With us."

"Weren't you going to let me make up my own mind? Some of those guys are practically family, too, you know." My parents both fell into a heavy, hurt silence. "Frank," Carol said. "What are you doing?" I needed to have private conversations with everyone, to go into the kitchen and close the door and invite them in one at a time to explain.

"You and the kids can meet some of my old buddies," I said. "Rhonda can hear me rockin' live and in person."

"Let's not make this worse," Carol said.

Rhonda had disappeared into her room once more. I wasn't sure when we'd see her again.

"This? What's *this?*" I said angrily. "A bad dinner, and suddenly . . ."

"What bad dinner?" my father said. "Your mother can barely walk."

"I'm not talking about walking," I said.

"Frank," Carol said. "Let's take a walk. I think we need to get out of the house."

"The boy can stay here with us," my mother said. "You'd like that, wouldn't you, boy?" My mother had forgotten his name. Or maybe she was figuring she'd never have to remember it.

"Danny, get your coat on," Carol said. "His name's Danny," she said to my mother.

"She knows what his name is," my father said.

Danny got his coat, and the Lillian Vernon Christmas scarf my mother had given him, and we were out the door.

We found a pile of plowed snow for Danny to climb on behind the little shopping center around the corner, and we moved far enough away so that he couldn't hear us.

"I've still got a lot of friends here. You'll like them. They want to meet you," I said. I made a snowball and threw it as far as I could.

"I don't care. I don't want to meet anyone else in your life here. I want you to take us back to Pittsburgh. You want to go off and play rock star again. I'm too old for this shit. I'm too old to sit and listen to your blowhard parents boss my kids around while you sit there stuffing your face with that awful turkey and pretending it's good! Why don't you pretend you actually like me instead? Huh, how about that?"

I could have or should have done a number of things then. Probably the dumbest thing I could've done was to walk them home, then get in my car and abandon Carol and Rhonda and Danny to a horrible night of silence with my parents to go play rock 'n' roll. But that's what I did. It sufficiently pissed everybody off, so that the next morning no one was talking to me, not even Danny.

■ ■ ■

Where were we going to have a private conversation in that tiny house? During breakfast, Carol kept looking at me across the room with a cross between a glare and the look of someone drowning. And I was sitting there with the guilty look of someone who'd shoved the women and children out of the way to jump into the lifeboat. The rooms in my parents' house were so tiny, the walls so thin, it was like one big room. We could take the kids out somewhere, but then we'd have to talk in front of them. I suppose I could've made some excuse for Carol and me to go out together alone, but I don't think either Carol or the kids wanted to be alone with my parents any longer. I didn't, either—with everything weighted, there was no telling what could be the wrong thing to say. I decided we'd just hit the road and deal with things back in Pittsburgh.

Why was I so worried about what my parents thought? I'd been so happy with Carol, and proud of her, of finding her, that I wanted some recognition for that. After disappointing my parents so often, I wanted to pleasantly surprise them. I wanted my dad to shake my hand as I walked out the door to drive back to Pittsburgh, to say in a low, sincere voice, "Frankie, you done good." I wanted my mother to embrace Carol and say, "Oh, dear, it was so good to meet you. Please take care of my boy."

Of course, it didn't happen that way. Carol and the kids sat in the car as it idled in the street and I stood in the doorway, my father shouting at me to shut the door because I was letting cold air in and my mother listlessly waving from across the room, disappointed one more time.

"It's not your fault," I said.

"Fault? For what? Of course it's not our fault!" my father said.

"I'll call," I said.

"You do that," my mother said.

I got in the car, and this time it was me who slammed the door twice. I wanted to slam my hand in it so I could scream. I knew better than to tell Carol it wasn't her fault.

On the way home, the bird clock chirped every hour from the trunk. I expected someone to say something—we could all hear it. But nobody said a word. Five hours, five birds. Saint Francis loved the birds—but even he wouldn't have wanted them mechanically chirping on the hour.

Saint Francis wanted to deny himself all pleasure as a way of getting closer to God. Saint Frank—he was the man. I mean, how could he just toss all his father's loot aside and go out in the woods to preach to the creatures? Saint Francis would've got down with Saint Clare if he weren't the messiah. He would've never learned how to drive. He would've never gotten himself stuck on the Ohio Turnpike. If his suitcase blew off the top of a car, he would've been grateful. With all the Catholic stuff shoved down my throat when I was a kid, Saint Francis appealed to me as an eccentric nut with a kind heart. My kind of messiah—hey, how about that for the name of a group?

■ ■ ■

On the ride home, everyone was quiet, even Danny. I felt like we'd attended a funeral, not Christmas. The ride on the turnpike always seemed longer than it actually was—the scenery and landscape never changed, just flat farmland and more flat farmland—but because of the traffic, this drive was even worse. Traffic was horrendous everywhere—around Toledo where they were redoing the drawbridge, at the turnpike tollbooths, in the gas line at the rest stop. Carol sat across from me, wedged against the door as far away as possible. I was worried my old Escort wouldn't make the trip and imagined us stranded in Ohio, as if our love was what had fueled the vehicle, and I'd siphoned it all out with my rock-band stunt.

I thought maybe we'd see some remnant of Rhonda's suitcase, but there was nothing. Carol and Rhonda stared out the windows. I don't know if they were looking for the suitcase, or for escape. Rhonda was having her period—she'd just started menstruating two months ago—so we stopped frequently. She was wearing new skin-tight jeans and a clingy top, her thin figure looking skeletal, almost malnourished. She was twelve, and she looked it in those teenage clothes, her face pale with pain and embarrassment.

She reminded me a little of myself at that age. I hated everybody, too, and my parents weren't even divorced, much less bringing strangers into my life that I was supposed to like. What was I doing with her mother? How long would I be in her life?

I had no answers for her. I was just the guy who'd let her suitcase blow away—one thing that she could've imagined was safe, contained. At least I could keep Danny amused by buying scratch-off lottery tickets outside the bathrooms. He won five dollars.

"We're rich," I said.

"What do you mean, *we*?" Carol said.

"Right. Keep your five dollars," I said. "Sorry."

Jill and I had lived together for two years without even seriously entertaining the notion of marriage. It didn't make any sense in our lives—we felt we were above all that official crap. I even wrote a song called "Just a Piece of Paper" for her. But now, as the Ohio Turnpike rolled beneath us, I saw that piece of paper drifting away from me and Carol, and I wanted to snatch it out of the air and sign on the dotted line. Was it all over between us? Perhaps I'd been trying to tie my life down with bungee cords when it didn't want to be tied down, or maybe I was just "stretching" a comparison. The Human Error broke up when our drummer punched our lead singer, though none of us seems to remember the cause of the fight.

You can actually get a decent cup of coffee at the new rest stops—we could have used that in the band days. Detroit, Cleveland, Pittsburgh. Erie, Youngstown, Flint. Sometimes D.C. or Baltimore. I spent so much time cramped in cars, sleeping in cars, taking turns driving all night, I would've been happy if I never had to drive ever again.

I'm not sure the band reunion is part of this story, but I have to admit I had a great time. It was amazing how quickly we came together again, the old songs permanently embedded in our memories. The warmth was palpable in old Saint Margaret's Hall, where we'd rehearsed when we were teenagers. I felt it as soon as Terry handed me a guitar. We knew we could never be those teenage punks again. We weren't dreaming of anything. Just playing music together and smiling and nodding at each other. Nobody had to be the front man. We weren't competing for anyone's attention. I wanted Carol and the kids to see me like that. It was where I always went to get away from my parents, and they should have gotten away with me. The guys wanted to do it again next year. They made me promise to bring Carol and her kids next time.

■　■　■

As we drove across Ohio, I wrote my first song in years, composing it in my head:

THE OHIO TURNPIKE BLUES

Not a decent cup of coffee
between here and Cleveland
and we've got 300 more miles
me and my band

A van full of guitars, mikes, and amps
gonna make it to Pittsburgh, PA
gonna show them all we're the champs
when we plug in and play

Rotten burgers, stale smoke, greasy fries
we got to make it there alive
wheels spinning over this flat land
but me and the boys, we got a plan

We're gonna make it big across the Midwest
this gig in Pittsburgh's gonna be the big test

But we got 300 more miles
me and my band
not a decent cup
not a decent cup
not a decent cup of coffee
between here and Cleveland

Lost a suitcase full of coke
along this breezy road
dealers they came after me
but I disappeared like smoke

I've come clean now
before the Lord and the Law
I'm coming clean now
with a black eye and busted jaw

Driving the Ohio Turnpike
I saw my life before me
black tracks leading nowhere
was all I could see

I vow to stay between the yellow lines
I vow to love my woman 'cause she's so fine
I vow to play my guitar in Pittsburgh, PA
'cause I don't live for tomorrow
I live for today

Not a decent cup of coffee
between here and Cleveland
and we've got 300 more miles
me and my band

The road's flat and straight
the boys are restless in the back
the drive's the part we hate
but it's not the drive we lack

We're plugged in now
and we're gonna rock ya
we're plugged in and how
and we're gonna boogie
we're plugged in now

and we're done roaming
we're plugged in now
and wherever we're plugged in
is home
we're home home home
and we're gonna rock
we're home home home
and we're gonna rock

Okay, so it's not Top 10 material. Or Top 1000 material. Whatever. I sang it aloud as we crossed the border into Pennsylvania, and they all giggled—Rhonda, Carol, Danny. They all guffawed—at me, not with me, but I was taking what I could get.

■　■　■

Danny smiled up at me as I helped him out of the car. I took his hand and immediately saw he was clutching the shepherd. "Lamb of God, take away the sins of the world," I recited. I still remembered half the mass—it was stuck there with all the bad song lyrics I ever wrote. I knew my parents would notice the missing shepherd when they carefully boxed up the decorations. I let Danny keep it. I figured I'd probably be coming home alone next year. Maybe I could surprise them with a new one.

I got the remaining suitcases down from the roof. Rhonda hurried inside and turned on the answering machine. I could hear its loud crackling as her father's voice wished them all a Merry Christmas—"Even you, Carol," he said with a laugh.

Most of the band breakups involved somebody storming out of a room with his instrument and never coming back. I don't remember anybody storming off to *join* a band, but that's what I'd done to Carol and the kids. Drummers rarely quit any of the bands, and I think it was because they couldn't make a dramatic exit with all that equipment to pack up. Jill had packed up and moved out while I was out on the road with the Human Error.

I was happy to have the chore of removing the suitcases, the complex bungee system that had to be dismantled. Carol and I carried their suitcases into the house. We had earlier made New Year's Eve plans together. Neither of us had said anything in front of the kids about backing off, or breaking up. Now was the chance, as we stood together in the cold, gray street lit by Christmas lights, light-up Frostys and Santas.

"I'm sorry for being a jerk," I said.

"I'm just so tired," she said. We stood together watching each other's breath.

"So, is this it?" I asked.

"Is this what?" Carol asked.

"Well, the whole trip was a disaster."

She came closer to me. "Disaster's a relative term, you know," she said. "I think we'll all live."

"'Disaster is a relative term.' Definite song possibilities. Lots of rhymes for 'term.'"

"I used to love to watch you play," she said. "You seemed to be having so much fun. I envied you up on stage."

I was so cold that I couldn't help but pull her into my open leather jacket. She hesitated, then curled inside it and wrapped her arms around my chest.

"All our suitcases should've blown away," she said.

"It's not so flat here," I said.

"Like in Ohio and Detroit," she said.

"More exits here," I said.

"More bridges," she said.

United States Street Football

The flat, crumbling streets of our subdivision were laid out in a basic, unimaginative grid except for the odd twist where Rome Street turned into Pearl Street and vice versa, crisscrossing like the passing routes we ran in the middle of the street in front of our house on Rome. We played two-hand *shove,* not two-hand touch. This was in large part due to Angelo Diogenes' habitual protestation of "You only got me one hand!" Our only alternative was to shove him into a parked car or, if he was lucky, over the curb onto the grass, in order to emphasize the second hand. But the day Angelo was hit by Pete Barone's speeding Pontiac Firebird and slo-mo'd his way up into the air and bounced off the windshield, as Pete swerved and kept going, a police car in hot pursuit, we had to change the rules once again and forever.

The *Free Press* reported that the accident occurred on Pearl, and of course they were wrong. No reporter even came out to look at the sparkling sweep of broken windshield glass. If we hadn't witnessed it ourselves, we could have half-imagined that the glass was evidence of simple vandalism and that Angelo would soon be showing up at our side doors with his scuffed-up football clutched in his arm, calling us out for another game of United States Street Football. The paper's story was all about Pete Barone, who eventually ran aground in the weedy, ambiguous yard of the old farmer and his wife, who at one time had farmed the entire neighborhood before selling it off to developers. The piece of land they were left with was never clearly defined—did they own the empty field behind the house? The vacant lot next door? All that was certain was that they were dying, were nearly dead. And they were scared out of their minds by the sirens and flashing lights of the emergency vehicles tearing ruts into their weedy yard. I never saw either of them ever again.

Pete had nearly killed his girlfriend, Donna Monaco, earlier that afternoon, smashing in her head with a blunt object that was never found, though we all guessed it was the billy club Pete had made in shop class the previous year before he dropped out. A billy club hollowed out and filled with lead. In Wood and Metal Shop at Warren Woods High School, the craft of weapon making was honed and refined under the bleary, bloodshot eyes of Mr. Ernie Cook, who in the imagined privacy of his adjacent office drank himself into oblivion every afternoon. The drunker and/or more hungover Ernie was, the more oil he put on his slicked-back hair, as if, if he just oiled it enough, some would sink through to kick-start his brain, or maybe simply relieve the endless headache of his life.

■ ■ ■

While it's not true that we blamed all our troubles on the blacks from Detroit, they were a convenient target, since none of us actually knew any black people. Our neighborhood was 50 percent Polish Catholic and 50 percent Southern Redneck. One hundred percent white. All the rumbles in our neighborhood, brutal as they were, were just scrimmages for the battles with blacks we imagined having. Though they never took place. Borders were respected. While we imagined they were threatening to cross Eight Mile Road and "invade" our neighborhood, in reality we had little they would have wanted. The one place where the races mixed was at the factory, and according to our fathers, even there, the departments were segregated.

Pete had claimed he'd made the club to hit random black people who might inadvertently stray across Eight Mile, but he'd ended up using it on Donna. Donna, one of the most beautiful dark-eyed foxes to ever sashay the sidewalks of Warren. I cringed, imagining her destroyed face as she lay in a coma at Marigold Hospital. Angelo dead and Donna Monaco vegetized—all because Pete Barone found out that Matt Ropp drove her home from a high school dance while Pete was pumping gas at Davey's Eight Mile Brake Service.

"Man," I said to my brother Steve. "Why can't Pete just back his car up all the way to his house and it could still be third down?" Steve was ten. I was thirteen.

"Transmission problems," Steve said. The one thing we all knew about was cars. How they worked, how they didn't work. What kind we were going to drive someday. We had already stopped riding bicycles, thinking they were for little kids, though for at least a couple more years, we had no alternative except to walk, or to hope some older guy would take mercy on us. Which Pete had done on many occasions, letting a gang of us pile into his Firebird and cruise the streets and smoke cigarettes, giving us that harsh burn in our throats we associated with getting older. It was really messing with our heads that our hero had gone and run down our friend and done a horrible thing to a beautiful girl. I'm still trying to figure out what happened to Pete Barone. And to us. For we all aspired to be Pete Barone. Though it is true that most kids in other neighborhoods aspired to kick Pete's ass instead, he was our Pete, and we had been his loyal followers.

Steve picked at his fingernails crusted with dirt, the peculiar black grit that collected against the curbs of our neighborhood, some obscure residue from the GM plant down on Ryan Road. I'd seen him collecting small, shiny pieces of safety glass from the street. Neither of us had spoken Angelo's name, even when we went to the funeral. *The* funeral, we called it. Not Angelo's funeral. We never said "Angelo," and we never said "dead."

■　■　■

Sometimes we got rides from Ricky Arnold, but Ricky was such a homely dork that he never knew where to drive us. He wanted us to be his pals, and that was creepy. Pete was aloof. He had style. "Now get out of here, you runts," he'd say to us, dropping us off on some random corner when he saw a cute girl he wanted to pick up.

We'd taken to bombing Ricky's car with iceballs during the winter. He drove a lame little Volkswagen Beetle. He was never going to catch us, so we could afford to be mean. Meanness and cruelty were generally valued, fell under the umbrella of being "tough." Tough luck. Tough titty. Tough. You had to be tough. I never heard my father use the word "sensitive." It had too many soft syllables, too little substance.

■　■　■

The day after the accident and before the funeral was endless. My father went to work, like any other day. My mother spent the morning in hushed tones on the telephone. Mr. Glabicki, who lived next door to Angelo's house, raised his American flag. His solution to anything was to fly the flag. He viciously hoarded our balls that landed in his yard, and barked like a dog if we set one foot on his perfect lawn.

"Well, God bless America," my mother said sarcastically when she looked out the window and saw the flag. "Asshole," she said under her breath.

I didn't want to leave the house and see any of the other guys, but I didn't want to stick around the house, either. Steve and I shared a room. He was spending the day sitting on his bed and sorting old baseball cards into various configurations. I'd stopped collecting them, and so had Steve, but he had held on to his old ones, and maybe he was taking comfort in their worn familiarity. I'd given him my old ones a couple of years back, and I felt a strange pang of jealousy watching him handling them, lost in some secret world.

They hadn't yet built the Bronco Lanes bowling alley on the field where we played baseball, and that's where I went—one of two seminatural spaces left in the neighborhood, a field that had been leaped over in the rush to develop the land around the factories more than thirty years earlier. Maybe the farmer hadn't sold that one odd piece out of some perverse loyalty to the land, or maybe somebody with a dream had bought it and was stubbornly holding on to the land, even though the dream itself had become abandoned and weeded over. I wandered through the hard, brittle weeds of October, kicking stray rocks. The wind, with nothing to block its path, barreled over the flat land and stung my face, penetrated my thin fall jacket.

Part of being tough meant that you didn't bundle up for cold weather. You jammed your fists into your jeans and said, "Fuck, it's cold," but you took it. You wiped your nose on your sleeve and cupped your red ears in your hands, but you took it. I kicked the ground again, and a heavy, waterlogged ball from some previous season emerged (we still occasionally smacked the ball around back there), and it rolled briefly away from me. I picked it up and hurled it as hard as I could, though it landed harmlessly, well short of Ryan. When we played then, Tony Bruno had to bat left-handed so he wouldn't hit it out into the traffic on Ryan. It seemed like we were outgrowing everything all at once.

■ ■ ■

Our neighborhood was so bland and anonymous that the Pearl/
Rome confusion was a source of pride—our one claim to fame, to
live on the street that changed names. On the other side of "the
woods"—our other natural space, an undeveloped patch behind
Pioneer Metals—Rome and Pearl continued briefly, then stopped
at Dequindre, the next big road parallel to Ryan. If you want to
figure it out, just draw a square. Ryan and Dequindre are on two
sides, and Eight Mile Road and Nine Mile Road the other sides. This
story is in that square mile, for if you lived outside that square, we
didn't know you. It's called South Warren in a disparaging way. A
euphemism for white trash, though we didn't consider ourselves
trashy. White, though. Definitely white. Three trailer parks were
located within that square mile. A lot of people trying to get over
the invisible speed bump of class and into a clean, new life with
lots of space around it. Invisible but enormous. All the horsepower
in the world wasn't going to get them over it.

Occasionally, some stranger would stop and roll down a window
to ask, "Boys, am I on Rome or Pearl?" To give bad directions—that
was a big thrill. Angelo was our best improviser. He'd hitch up his
pants, lean over the window, and direct some poor stranger into the
bowels of suburbia. We couldn't get them too lost, since we lived so
close to Eight Mile. Everybody knew Eight Mile, the border between
Detroit and Warren—we couldn't send them in that direction—but
if we kept them on the identical, anonymous side streets, they'd be
busy for a while. Sometimes they'd even circle back to us, angrily
stopping to curse as we scattered.

Scattering was difficult in our neighborhood, whether you were
on foot, on bike, or behind the wheel of a car. When everything is
squared off, where are the shortcuts? Pete'd tried to take a shortcut
to revenge. Why didn't he go after Matt Ropp in a fair fight? The

Pete we knew would never bash in a girl's head. But the Pete we knew never existed—he was the exhaust fumes of our imagination.

Fence climbing was a revered art form in our neighborhood. Pete had been a championship fence climber. He'd needed that skill often, since he frequently found himself escaping some irate father or a mob of teenagers from another neighborhood. Pete could push himself up and swing his legs over in one easy motion, while the rest of us were busy sticking our feet in and out of gaps between the wire mesh to get ourselves up and over the bar while some mad dog nipped at our pant legs.

I believe Pete had some special dog thing going. The same dogs that would tear their teeth through my pant legs as I tried to escape would just wag their tails and watch Pete, almost as if they were hoping he'd stop to chat, or pat them on the head or something. Dog eat dog. Dog meat. Pete was dog meat now. If we'd had the chance, we would have swarmed over him like mad birds or killer bees, swarmed over him and brought him down. Some of us had made our own clubs.

■ ■ ■

United States Street Football was a league we created of twelve three-man teams. There were only eight players in the league—me, Ralph, Tony, Angelo, Jimbo, Paz, Stan, and Ziggy—so we were all on more than one team. This made scheduling particularly difficult, but we'd developed a complicated set of rules for substitutions and exceptions that no one ever wrote down but that we all carried in our heads more firmly than any math facts from school. Sometimes friends from the fringe would join in, substituting for someone who was supposed to be on both teams. We called them Special Guest Stars. Steve played when we let him. Three years' age difference doesn't seem like much, but back then it was a completely separate generation. Once, we got Pete to play. He would only play quarterback, at least in part because he was wearing his shit-kicker boots and couldn't run very well. To make things fair, we made him quarterback for both teams. Pete liked to throw as hard as he could, even if it was just a short safety valve pass over the middle. He just about caved in my sternum with one of those. There were short bombs and long bombs, but everything was a bomb.

We'd painted yard lines on the street and "U.S.S.F." on the fifty-yard line, which got some of the neighbors really pissed off, but the cops who came out to investigate seemed to get a kick out of it. We did it as professionally as we could, but it was late at night, and we were nervous about cars, so the paint was a little wobbly in places. The cops just laughed, got back in their car, and drove off.

We weren't big on uniforms—we knew who was on what team. We had shirts scrawled with team names that we sometimes remembered to wear. It's not like we were going to get confused. None of us wanted to be on teams with uniforms and pads, where everybody got the same haircut and coaches grabbed you by the face mask and spat in your face. In our league, everybody was a quarterback, receiver, or running back. No one had to disappear into an anonymous herd of blockers. We'd be disappearing into the factory in a few years, so we wanted to be stars while we could.

No goalposts, of course. Ten touchdowns won the game. I can't remember how we did extra points. Maybe it'll come to me later. Right now, I'm back on the street looking at Angelo's body splayed half on the curb, half in the street. The football's in my hands. The police car that's been chasing Pete swerves to a stop. We're all running to Angelo, then stopping short. The cops seem briefly torn between continuing pursuit and helping him. They radio something, then push their way to the body. "The boy." "Hurt bad." "No pulse." Panicked doors are swinging open, mothers emerging from houses, drawn by the squealing tires and the awful thump. None of us touches Angelo's body. The mothers are running. They will do what needs to be done. We are ants attracted and repelled, confused by the dead body in the path of our short lives. It's Angelo. Angelo. And there's his mother, the only divorcée on the street back then. Angelo is her *man*. "My little man." She's screaming as if she is on fire, screaming and sprinting the length of the street like the sirens we're hearing in the distance, approaching. His mother struggling with one of the cops. Twisting, pounding on his chest. Young cops, scared. "No pulse." They let her through. "Back up, everyone. Back up. Now!" I'm holding the football. Me, Ralph, Tony, Jimbo, Paz. Backing up. Our mothers grabbing us, separating us. Pete. Everybody knew Pete. Pete's mother. There she is. There she goes. You didn't have to say his last name. Wailing and tears, but not mine. Angelo. Dead. Angelo dead. His football. A present from his rarely seen father. Almost new. In my hands. Dragged away to our porch. "Stay there!" my mother shouts, but I go to Ralph's, and we stand. Together. Not a word. The ambulance takes Angelo and his mother. The crowd sprays into ugly clusters.

Everyone knew Pete's Firebird. Some go to the next block to look at the wreck, the next cluster of vehicles. Siren City. U.S.S.F, "Who let those kids paint this?" somebody who doesn't know Rome from Pearl asks accusingly. "We did." Angry mother. "We did. So?"

My statement: "We were playing football. He was going on a post pattern. The car swerved around the corner going a hundred miles an hour and hit him." I can't say his name. I have nothing else to say. My mother sits with me on the couch, her arm around me. I do not complain. I begin then. To cry. And cry. And cry. Football in my arms.

■ ■ ■

Around Halloween the previous year, we'd tied a dummy to a long rope and tossed it up over the streetlight. We hid in the bushes and dropped the dummy on passing cars. We nailed Pete's. It scared the shit out of him, and he was pissed off. But once he calmed down, he appreciated the quality of the prank. "Nice one, punks," he said, then got back into his car and squealed away. I can't remember if Angelo was with us that night. The dummy didn't last long. Those long drops ripped it open after a few free falls. Sometimes the truth is so bizarre you don't stand a chance of anyone believing it. The sound—the sound was a lot different.

■ ■ ■

"Well," Ralph said. Or "Hell." He lived next door, so I saw him the most. He was one year older. A week after Angelo's funeral, and we were tired of sitting around in our houses after school, even though our mothers had let us watch all the TV we wanted. Homework seemed pointless, and the teachers were cutting us slack. We didn't want any more slack. We wanted to play. But our parents had decided against any more U.S.S.F. The paint lines weren't going away, but we weren't allowed.

The schedule was not mentioned. The final standings were not mentioned. I had stuffed Angelo's ball under my bed. I didn't think his mother would want it. She had been led off by an old aunt to live in her house in Hazel Park, on the other side of Dequindre, and there was no telling when or if she was coming back. My mother sent us down to rake the leaves from her yard. The Diogenes' was one of the few houses on the block that did not have a garage, for when the garage builders were coming through the neighborhood, Angelo's parents were already divorced. That's why he was the only only-child on the block—his parents hadn't stuck together long enough to have more than one.

I let Ralph's "Well" or "Hell" hang there for a while. I was still smelling Mrs. Diogenes' heavy perfume from when she hugged me at the funeral, still dizzy with the spinning nightmare of the past ten days.

"Yeah. What are we gonna do now?" I said finally. The end of October, and getting too cold to sit on the porch like we were doing. My nose was running, and I wiped it on the back of the sweatshirt I'd scrawled "Raiders" on. When I turned it inside out, it said "Spartans."

"Where's the ball?" None of the rest of us had a ball, unless you counted Paz's undersized rubberized yellow football that we used in emergencies. It was always going to be an emergency from now on, but that didn't mean we couldn't play.

"I'll go get it." I ran home and crawled under my bed. The ball was dusty, so I rubbed it clean. Dusty already. I ran back out and threw a long pass to Ralph, who jumped off his porch and caught it. "Touchdown!" I yelled, a little too loudly, as if I hadn't used my voice at all since the—we didn't know what to call it—the accident?

■ ■ ■

Pete's mother was the niece of the old farmer and his wife, so they'd move into one of the first houses in the development back in the mid-fifties, a corner house where Bruce bisected Pearl and Rome right where they crisscrossed. Pete was the oldest kid in the neighborhood, and that had given him added status to begin with. He was charged with vehicular homicide and attempted murder, and at least a half dozen other crimes I can't remember. He pleaded guilty, so none of us had to testify.

Pete's parents had appeared briefly at Angelo's funeral, hushing all motion, all tears. The funeral of a child is the worst funeral in the world. We didn't know that at the time—we thought they were all that bad. The raw grief overcoming the stiff, antiseptic artificiality of the funeral home. At least Angelo had a closed casket. Donna Monaco had an open casket for the rest of her life. Donna was still in critical condition, though her parents thought to send flowers for

Angelo. Flowers, useless flowers, overflowing the cramped rectangle of the "viewing room," a name I thought was creepy. I thought they would all be that bad, that they would all be that crowded, though I never saw a funeral home that packed ever again. It was at Molinski's funeral home over on Ryan. The police were out directing traffic, old man Molinski running back and forth from inside to outside to keep checking on things. He even forgot to put out his cigar before he came back in, and the trace smoke lingered like old shit among the perfume of the flowers.

■ ■ ■

On the other half of Rome, which was officially called Pearl, Donna Monaco recovered. Eventually. More or less. Permanent brain damage and facial scarring, but she survived. She could never go back to school or get a job or live on her own. She used to walk to church every morning with her mother, though I have no idea what they prayed for, either of them. We'd pass them on our way to school. We never even said hi, though they didn't seem to mind. We turned away or looked down—at least, I did—every single time. I don't know what her personality was like, when she had one, but I do know that before, she was incredibly beautiful, with long black hair that curled around her waist as she walked. Her features were sharp, and her eyes piercing and fierce. I always felt when I saw her that she was one girl who was going to do exactly what she wanted. Maybe even go to college, which was extremely rare in our neighborhood, no matter what street you lived on. I couldn't stand to see her looking like some stupid pet to be led by the hand. Her nose had been smashed in, and they could only do so much with it. Her hair was short—I guess to make it less trouble for her mother. Donna herself seemed incapable of caring about or dealing with her own appearance. It broke my heart to see her, and I was only thirteen, so when my heart broke, it broke pretty deep and with all sincerity. If she would have died, we all could have considered her a saint and gone on with our lives, but she lived, and lived, and lived.

■　■　■

Ralph and I started playing with Angelo's ball. We devised a game on the front lawn where the object was to throw the ball high enough so that you could run across the entire yard in time to catch it. Every play was a touchdown or an incompletion. That's the way it was in our neighborhood—you either made a touchdown and got out of there, or you were never quite fast enough and eventually settled down to a steady job in the factory, where you blocked for the big stars, whoever and wherever they were. Knowing it was Angelo's ball spooked me. I was torn between seeing it as a precious treasure and seeing it as a flying nightmare of my dead friend. I suddenly turned and hurled it over the low roof of the house, where I knew it would land harmlessly in the backyard. Perhaps it would roll into a pile of dog shit, but that could be wiped off.

"Let's get out of here," I said to Ralph, and he didn't ask where. He just followed in step beside me, and we wandered off, passing the three houses of our tragic trinity—Pete's, Donna's, and Angelo's, the three neglected yards, the three porches with white paint curling into strips and falling to the ground. No matter who lives in those three houses, for us they'll always be Pete's, Donna's, and Angelo's. "Let's get out of here," I said again later, as we stood back in front of our houses where we had started.

I was thirteen, so maybe I didn't know what I was talking about, but Ralph didn't question that, either. Maybe he nodded silently before we went back into our separate houses. Mr. Glabicki got a petition started to straighten out the street names so Rome would stay Rome and Pearl would stay Pearl, but for the people who would be affected, it was too late. Mr. Glabicki lived alone, had always lived alone, so what did he know? Him and his goddamn flag. Him and his goddamn war medals. Rome and Pearl, Pearl and Rome. Hesitation corner. Engine idling. Somebody scratching his head, rolling down a window. Somebody politely asking for a way out. They weren't going to get a straight answer from any of us.

The year after the accident, somebody put a small cross in the Rutalskis' lawn near where Angelo had landed, but it was gone the next day. Nobody wants a cross like that on their front lawn, do they? When Pete's name did come up, we called him Barone. He wasn't Pete anymore. I got rid of my billy club, burned it with the trash one night out behind the garage, though it took a while. Everything took a while. The paint slowly eroded from the U.S.S.F. so that by the time we were driving our own cars, the faint white smudges could have been anything.

Ralph was our statistician, and he held on to the scribbled records on the wrinkled, rain-streaked—or tear-streaked?—pieces of paper. We could drive there now, to that same house, knock on the door, and Ralph would pull them down from an old shoe box and lay them out for us, explaining how to make twelve teams out of eight players, Angelo's name on the sheets circled, surrounded by stars, wherever it appears.

One day that February, Ricky Arnold beeped his horn at us, and we didn't throw anything at him, though there were plenty of chunks of ice handy from the plowed A&P parking lot. He pulled over to the curb and opened the passenger door, and we piled in.

No Man's Land

Jack knew he shouldn't put the whole wad of gum in his mouth, but he was twelve years old and knew that any step backward was an admission of defeat, a plunge back into childhood. He struggled to soften it up before he choked or suffocated. He lowered his head so his friends couldn't observe his struggle. It had cost him a dime for the Big Wad—no false advertising there—a slab of bubble gum thick as a deck of cards. And he was going to be stupid enough to chew it all at once to try to impress his friends.

"Hey, Jackie, how about sucking *my* Big Wad?" Ed Holder said, grabbing his crotch. Ed was thirteen, yet shorter than the others—held back once, but no dummy. Jack hadn't thought of that—everything was turning into some euphemism or double entendre for sex. And his mouth was so full he had no opportunity for the witty rejoinder. He garbled out, "Fuck you," with so little clarity that he could have been saying "Harpoon" or "Kung fu." Yet everyone knew what he had intended, so when Ed gave him an aggressive shove, it was no surprise.

They were standing on the cement in front of Ritter's Variety Store at Eight Mile and Ryan among the candy wrappers and empty cigarette packs clicking and scattering across the concrete like drunken mice in the strong, cold breeze. Jack took out the misshapen wad of gum and whipped it at Ed's head: direct hit. The others—Tall, Steve, and Junior—simultaneously laughed and backed away. Ed charged at Jack. It was a conspicuous place for a fight. If they'd been serious about it, they would have drifted into the alleyway beside Ritter's and sincerely duked it out, but Jack and Ed had such a long history together that deep inside, where nobody talked about, they didn't want to hurt each other. The casual observer, such as Mr. Ritter, would not have seen it that way. As they punched and wrestled in their thick winter coats, Mr. Ritter was calling the police.

So it was that at three o'clock on a dim Saturday afternoon in December, Jack had to get out of a police car in front of his parents' house and explain why. Why he had gotten into a fight about bubble gum at age twelve.

■ ■ ■

Jack and Ed, at opposite ends of the backseat of the police car, sullenly answered the officer's questions. Jack was snorting blood back up his nose, trying to keep up appearances. Trying not to burst into tears and cry, "I want my mommy," and blow it for the rest of his life.

The police officer offered them each a stick of gum, and the two boys glanced at each other and inexplicably began snickering. That might've gotten him mad enough to take them to the station and lock them up for a while, have their parents pick them up there, but upon laughing, Jack released all the blood he was holding in, and it came streaming out of his nose in a large gush.

"Damn it, now look what you done," Officer Friendly said. He scrambled around under his seat and came up with a greasy hand towel that he pushed through the mesh between the seats. Ed pulled it through and handed it to Jack, who squeezed it against his face, inhaling oil and antifreeze. "Let's get you boys home before you mess up my car any more." The other boys, shooed away by Friendly and Mr. Ritter, stood together over by the A&P and watched. As soon as Friendly pulled away, Jack saw them sprinting awkwardly over the dirty snow back toward their neighborhood—to spread the hot news on a cold December day.

■ ■ ■

They were always waiting for something to happen in their neighborhood in Warren, just outside Detroit. Detroit, known for its violence and danger, got all the headlines. Whenever a police car cruised down their street, they'd follow it on their bikes to see where it was going to land—when it landed at Ed's house, he'd peel off from the group and disappear. There were always two cops then. Jack's older brother, Mel, told him they sent two for domestic disputes—one for the husband, one for the wife. The Holders had the most decrepit house on their block of tiny three-bedroom boxes built for autoworkers in the fifties. The shabbiness of the outside reflected the inner turmoil that revealed itself in the occasional loud thumps and screams, and in Mrs. Holder's purple, swollen face the time they took Mr. Holder away in handcuffs.

Now something had happened, and it had happened to Jack. Everybody would be surprised, particularly his parents. Ed had turned pale and silent next to him, perhaps imagining the reaction of his own parents. Jack thought he'd prefer staying with the cop to entering the Holders' house at that moment, though soon enough his parents would drag him there. As the policeman led him up the sidewalk, Jack could see his father in front of the TV watching some college hoops, drinking a slow Saturday afternoon beer.

■ ■ ■

Jack and Ed sat on the thin, lumpy couch in the Holders' drab front room that served as both living and dining room. The TV was off. Their parents gathered around the table.

"They were fighting about gum, can you believe it?" Ed's mother, Sophie, said.

"Let the boys tell it," Jack's father, Ron, said, holding up his hand. Bobby, Ed's father, wordlessly left the table and came back with four long-neck Stroh's, opened them, and set them in front of each adult like a ceremonial candle.

"I'm pregnant," Jack's mother, Rachel, said, stating the obvious. Bobby just slid her bottle next to his own without a word. Jack noticed the tight, thick rope of his neck, as if there was a permanent strain there, a permanent bad taste or stuck bone of anger. Bobby was short, like his son, but, unlike Ed, he rarely spoke. Ed got the chattiness from Sophie, who couldn't seem to help herself.

Jack was scared, but he didn't want to get Ed in more trouble by repeating the off-color insult.

"We were just goofing around," Ed said, his voice rising up at the end as if he were unsure, trying it out to see if it floated.

"Fooling around doesn't bring you home in the back of a cop car," Ron said, turning his chair and leaning toward the boys. Bobby was silent, leaning back, sucking down a beer, one leg pumping up and down off the floor.

"It started out fooling around," Jack put in.

"I'll never be able to show my face in Ritter's again," Sophie chimed in from her distant planet. Jack knew from Ed that Ritter's wouldn't give their family any more credit—she'd lost face in Ritter's a long time ago.

"Just shut up," Bobby said, whipping his neck around to face his wife.

Ron flinched, glanced at Rachel, and tried again.

"Let the boys tell it," Ron said again softly, looking at Sophie, who looked at Bobby, who looked away.

Jack had wanted to cry for hours but had held it in. Now the tears were sliding down his cheeks. Rachel began to slowly get to her feet to go to him, but Ron gently held her back. Jack's stomach was hollow with hunger yet filled with the heavy stone of shock. He felt as if a firecracker had gone off unexpectedly in his hand. Like he needed to count his fingers and assess the damage. He wished his ears would stop ringing.

■ ■ ■

One night a couple of years earlier, Ed had slept over at Jack's. Ed had been bugging Jack about a sleepover, though he himself had never even asked Jack inside his house—it was clearly a forbidden subject between them, as if his house did not exist, as if he just disappeared each night while the other boys went into real houses. When the policeman had asked Ed his address, he'd hesitated and stumbled over it.

When Jack's mom told them to put on their pajamas, Ed came out of the bathroom in his briefs. He didn't have pajamas. He slept in his underwear at home.

"What are you doing?" Jack asked. Ed's underwear was faded gray, stained yellow.

"You can't walk around our house in those," Jack's mother said. She quickly hurried to her room and grabbed a robe. "Here, put this on." It was her powder-blue quilted robe.

Ed blushed, but his face twisted, then hardened. "I can't wear this." Jack laughed. His mother frowned. Ron came back into the hallway, and he laughed, too. They asked Ed to put his clothes back on until bedtime—though bedtime was another issue. Ed didn't have a bedtime, he claimed.

Jack lay in the top bunk, Ed beneath him, where Mel usually slept.

"Wow, these are cool beds," Ed said. "I feel like I'm in a cave or something . . ." Just as Jack was drifting off, he felt his arm being jerked from below.

"Hey," Ed said in a loud whisper. "Your dad ever belt you?"

"He just sends me to my room when he's mad," Jack mumbled.

"He sends you in here? What punishment is that?"

"It gets boring. There's nothing to do."

"I'd take being sent to my room any time."

Jack didn't want to hear about it. He knew, everybody on the street knew, that the Holders' was a violent house. He let the silence hang there, and again he began to drift.

"Any time." Ed repeated. Then he reached up and yanked Jack's arm and pulled him down off the bed. Jack hit his head hard against the floor, and his parents came running. Ed sat smirking in his safe place while Rachel comforted Jack.

In the middle of the night, while prowling the house alone, Ed turned on the garbage disposal, jolting Jack awake, the grinder howling through the night's silence. Ed set off alarms wherever he went—and Jack loved him and hated him for it.

In the morning, Ed wolfed down an enormous stack of pancakes, then threw up on the kitchen floor. As morning lengthened toward noon, he wouldn't leave. "Isn't it time you headed home, Ed? Aren't your parents worried about you?" Jack's parents hinted. Ed stayed past lunchtime, though Jack's parents refused to feed him any more, fearing he'd be sick again. Later, Jack heard his parents joking that they were worried Ed's parents had picked up and left town, that they'd be stuck with him forever.

Jack liked Ed for contradictory reasons. One, Ed always made him look good in comparison. And two, Ed's sense of anarchic play was never boring. Everybody was more alive with Ed around—Ed, thin, spindly, manic, flashing an infectious grin. Like a mistreated dog, he winced if anyone came too close, but he was always creeping closer when you weren't looking.

■ ■ ■

"The whole thing is just stupid," Ron said finally.

Sophie glared at him. "That's one thing we agree on."

"You're grounded for . . . until further notice. A long time," Ron said.

"Until the baby comes," Rachel said. She was due in a month. "Then I'll want you out of my hair for a while. Now, let's go home."

Jack himself felt both slightly insulted and slightly relieved. He turned to glance at Ed as he stood, following his parents' example. Ed was staring into his hands.

"That sounds about right," Ron said. "You boys look so scared, I think you've had plenty of punishment already. Right, Bobby?"

"What?" Bobby said. Jack noticed the line of empty bottles on the floor next to his chair, five dead soldiers. Five little submissive pets. On the table sat a pint bottle of whiskey he'd been sipping from.

"What about me?" Ed asked.

Bobby looked at Jack's parents. "Appreciate you coming over. Now, we've all had a long day." He walked past them to the door and handed them their coats.

"Sure you have to leave so soon?" Sophie asked, as if they'd just paid a friendly social call. Jack wondered if they were the first neighbors to see the inside of their house.

"We'll talk soon," Rachel replied, patting Sophie's shoulder. "Under better circumstances, I hope." She shot a quick glance at Bobby's back. His black, slicked-back hair shone with grease in the hallway light.

■ ■ ■

Six eighth graders and four fifth graders lived on their block, but Jack and Ed were the only sixth graders. They'd been linked together by shared classrooms and playgrounds ever since Ed had been held back after first grade. Even though Jack spent more time with Ed than any other friend, he never counted Ed as his *best* friend. Though Ed was always around—one summer, after he began habitually showing up every morning, Jack's mother had to tell Ed not to come over unless invited—he never seemed to show Jack any affection or loyalty. Sometimes it seemed like he just needed someone to pick a fight with. When they parted, the feeling Jack had most often was simply relief.

A slight taint of badness was associated with the entire Holder family. During the school year, Jack spent much less time with Ed—his school friends clearly saw Ed as a loser—"white trash." But each summer, their friendship rekindled out of boredom and proximity.

The previous summer, Jack had erected his father's old canvas house tent in the backyard. Ed had been arriving at their door every day again. Bobby was out of work, and most days he sat brooding on the porch, occasionally barking at Sophie or Ed to bring him something or to shut up. The other kids in the neighborhood started crossing the street just to pass their house.

Jack's parents let Ed sleep over in the tent one hot, humid August night. Had even suggested it, which left Jack completely baffled. "Why don't you invite Ed to sleep over? You boys could have some fun out there. . . . Just don't go roaming the streets. Don't let Ed talk you into anything crazy," Ron had said. Lying on top of their sleeping bags, they stripped down to their underwear, but it never cooled down. The humidity hung like warm spit in the air. They played with their flashlights, creating monsters on the canvas walls.

As the light passed over Ed's scrawny torso, Jack saw discolored bruises on Ed's neck and shoulders. He made a shadow rabbit with his fingers, and it hopped across the dark world. Later, with every light in every house on the block completely dark, Jack and Ed sprinted naked around the block. They had dared each other.

Jack didn't trust Ed to open the gate quietly, so he slowly lifted it himself, and off they ran, their feet slapping against cement. It was slightly cooler outside the tent, and their own bodies created a slight breeze. Jack didn't remember ever running so fast. When they turned from Rome onto Bruce, they saw a car's headlights angling around the corner, and they dove into some bushes, scratching their chests on the prickly branches.

As they continued down Bruce to Otis, Otis to Bach, and Bach back to Rome, Jack lengthened the distance between himself and Ed. He turned back to see Ed with his arms raised above his head, stumbling forward. Ed had no wind—skin tight over his ribs, he looked like a dancing ghost. Jack kept going, then dove into the yard, through the open tent flap, and down onto his sleeping bag again. He winced when he heard the gate clang shut. Then Ed dove in, laughing hysterically. Soon, they heard Jack's father's voice through the back window.

"You boys be quiet out there, you hear?"

"Yeah, Dad," Jack said, stifling his own laughter as Ed rolled around the canvas floor like a deranged monkey or simply a boy released from his cage of fear.

■　■　■

The bitter wind blew snow sideways across their path as they hit the sidewalk and turned right, down the block to their own house. Jack scrambled for a place near his parents, though the sidewalk was only wide enough for two, so he zigzagged across the sidewalk in front of them, full of relief to be out in the open air, snow swirling around him.

"Oh, man," Ron said. He wrapped his burly arm around Rachel's shoulder, leaving no room for Jack between them. "I think we might be seeing the cops on the street again real soon," he mumbled under his breath.

Jack caught his father's voice on the wind. He now understood why his parents had hurried him down to Ed's house so quickly after the police had dropped him off—to try to prevent what might be happening right now in the Holders' house behind them.

"Maybe we should just go ahead and call the police," Rachel said quietly.

"And tell them what?" Ron asked. He pulled his arm off his wife's shoulder. Jack expected his parents to be more concerned with *him,* to have more stern things to say.

"You know what he's going to do to that boy. Sophie, too—just for good measure."

Jack heard the long sigh of his father rise briefly above the wind. Cold smoke rising and disappearing. His nose ached. He felt his friend's blows once again and flinched. The streetlight in front of him on their front lawn continued idly flickering and flashing, as it had for the past week. Above them, the silent moon appeared between clouds to shine its evil eye on all of them.

■　■　■

Last summer, Ed had snuck some of his father's porno magazines out of the house to show Jack. Bobby caught him trying to sneak them back in. Jack didn't see Ed for a week. He had even taken the bold step of calling Ed's house. Sophie said Ed was sick. When Ed finally did emerge, his left eye was still discolored, purple and yellow, and nothing was said.

It was those silences, the unspoken things, that strained their friendship—not a bad joke about bubble gum. Jack didn't want to know what went on at the Holders', but he did know—knew enough—and that made him angry at Ed. He knew this was wrong, but he couldn't help it. He didn't want to be reminded of how screwed up people were, and every time he saw Ed now, he felt an odd chill, as if some of the tainted chaos of the Holder family might rub off on him.

Jack had looked at *Playboys* and *Penthouses* before, but nothing prepared him for the raw, lurid, naked bodies in Ed's father's magazines. Ed had taken them to their hiding place between the old wooden fence and the cinder-block wall that separated their street from the tool-and-die shop behind them. For about six feet, the walls overlapped, creating a long private corridor. That narrow space was enough for a couple of standing bodies. You could also crouch, your back against the rough wood, feet braced against the gray brick. Though Ed and Jack rarely used that hiding space, it was something they shared—a place for secrets and escape.

Each magazine had a theme: S&M, threesomes, women with enormous breasts, anal sex. In one, the women, when they were dressed, were wearing school uniforms. Everything was overly bright—too red, too pink, on the thick, glossy paper. The women looked drugged or disinterested. Jack noticed the magazines' outrageous prices: thirty dollars, fifty dollars. How could Mr. Holder afford them?

Ed stared at him expectantly as Jack flipped through the magazines. Jack felt a coldness creeping through his chest. It wasn't the excited thrill he got from looking at the soft-core magazines. He thought of Ed's grim, silent mother passing on her way to the grocery store and how she might be linked to these.

"Where'd you find them?"

"Rafters. In my dad's workroom."

"Don't they give you the creeps? Man . . . those women look like zombies or something. And some of that shit, man, I mean, why would anybody let somebody else tie them up or . . ."

Ed looked disappointed. It was as if he himself had no opinion of the magazines and was waiting for Jack to give him one. "Yeah, but aren't they cool? I mean, *Playboy* doesn't show them like that."

The extreme close-ups looked like they belonged in a textbook. For some other grade, for some advanced level. Jack thought about Ed's father fingering these magazines in the dark, dank basement. Every house on their street had the same layout, and all the basements flooded during rainstorms. Three bedrooms, one bath, tiny kitchen, square living and dining rooms, picture window, and a slab of cement for a porch. And in the basement of at least one of them, one man was flipping these pages. Or noticing their absence, and waiting for someone to bring them back.

■　■　■

Jack sat in his room for hours, staring at the flickering yellow light against the darkness at the window. His heart was still thumping in his ears. His parents had gone to bed, and the house was completely silent. He knew Ed was getting a beating. Would they ever be able to be friends again? Ed. Where could a kid like him go? Jack was grounded. He had to stay home.

Was Ed's father just pure evil? Why was he so mean? Jack tried to remember times when Bobby had been nice to Ed, or to him, to anyone on the street. Bobby was a pipe fitter, and he was often out of work, though the other men in the neighborhood seemed to hold on to their factory jobs except during big layoffs. One winter, Bobby'd shown a group of boys the proper technique for bumper hitching—grabbing onto a car bumper and catching a ride down a snow-covered street. Once, he'd given Jack's father a jump on the street. Ron worked for Ford as an electrician. He didn't spend a lot of time with Jack and Mel because he was always at work. But he never hit them, or threatened to hit them. He seemed more resigned to his place in the world than angry with it. Jack wished he liked Ed more. That he could take some clear heroic action.

Unable to sleep, Jack got dressed and snuck out of the house. As soon as he stepped outside, he felt relief, but as he walked toward Ed's house, he had trouble catching his breath. He sucked in the icy air. He hadn't been able to locate his black gloves or gray stocking hat in the dark, so his ears and fingers burned numb. A light was on in the Holders' living room—a small table lamp. Jack slowed down and tried to peer through the frosted window. Sophie sat unmoving. No TV glow. No book or magazine. She was staring into space.

Jack kept moving. He was already frozen, the wind rubbing his face with it. He liked the emptiness of night, quiet enough to hear the passing trains near Eight Mile and Mound. From streetlight glow to streetlight glow, he wandered. He looped past Bronco Lanes, where a cleaning service was busy inside—he could hear a vacuum cleaner. Weeds poked up through the snow in the gap between the bowling alley and the tool-and-die shop. Jack tried to step where no one had stepped yet, to make his footprints distinct. Suddenly, he knew where he was headed: the hiding place. He plowed his way through the high, untouched snow and slipped between the fences. Sheltered from the wind, he braced himself between a wall and a fence—two barriers, two defenses. He blew into his cupped hands and made a wish or said a prayer for the lost, and for the found.

Mr. Pleasant

Robin and I stood together in her tiny kitchen, our jeans slouching into each other in front of the rusty sink. She lived in an apartment above an abandoned storefront on Main Street in Big Rapids. There are no big rapids in Big Rapids, Michigan. Just as there are no mountains in Mount Pleasant, Michigan. At that moment, I couldn't remember her name. I kept thinking Sue, though I knew it was wrong. I closed my eyes for a minute, hoping it would come to me.

When I was a child, I misread the map and thought the town was *Mister* Pleasant. I was sorely disappointed when I discovered the truth, yet not enough to keep me from moving there to attend college at Central Michigan University. Maybe I was still hoping I'd find a Mr. Pleasant who'd be willing to cut me some slack. It was the only place that accepted me with my 2.1 GPA. It must have been that 0.1 that got me in—that A in Outdoor Chef my junior year. I was determined to get away from Detroit, and if it took college to get me there, so be it. The old man was paying.

"We're leaving now, Red," Matt Rumberg said. He stood behind me, his wife, Jean, behind him. I called them the Glumbergs, for

51

despite their willingness to go anywhere and do anything, they seemed unwilling to enjoy themselves, particularly when they were together. I was nicknamed Red for obvious reasons. My real name was Tim. Matt was my second cousin, and they'd needed help paying the rent, so I was living in their spare room. We'd driven out together on our friend Sam's promise of a good party. Two hours is a long way to drive just for a good party, but we were tired of the Central scene, and we hadn't seen Sam since he'd graduated the previous spring. He was now, to everyone's amusement, a drug counselor in Big Rapids. This was before all the drug testing, so you pretty much had to believe what people told you, and I still think that's the way it should be. Sam could counsel anybody on drugs.

I opened my eyes: her name was Robin. "Okay," I said, turning quickly back to her. Believing in a Mr. Pleasant—perhaps it was that kind of faith that allowed me to let my friends abandon me in Big Rapids, despite having no ride back to Mount P. I'd never slept with a Robin before. I was nearly finished shredding my last semester at Central. I blamed it on living on *West* Center Street. There was no plain old Center Street in Mount Pleasant, and that's where I needed to be.

■　■　■

The roads were slick, with snow on top and ice beneath. While we'd drifted back and forth across M-46, I occasionally dragged my boot on the ground out the open passenger door to make sure we were still on the road. When I hit gravel, I hollered, and Matt swerved back onto the road. Whenever a car passed us heading the other way, I closed my eyes. All for the promise of a good party. I loved parties, and I loved women. I loved women, and I loved parties. I loved the prospect of meeting women at parties. I was a coon hound for parties, could sniff one out and track it from miles away. *Mount* Rapids, *Big* Pleasant. Anywhere.

"This is a bad idea," Matt kept saying, but we arrived safely, got drunk, laughed with Sam, and danced among the random bouncing bodies. Pretty much just like a Mount P party, but the faces were different—a little older and more interesting. Robin was a second-grade teacher. While there was a sprinkling of college students from nearby Ferris State—Robin had invited her student teacher, and she'd brought friends—many of the partiers were older singles despairing over their singleness in a place that flat and desolate, in a place that offered few opportunities for coupling. There was a frenzy in the air to hook up. Like at a high school make-out party, people groped each other openly. Because they were older, they seemed more serious and purposeful about their drinking, and their groping. It was winter, and nobody seemed to want to leave just one set of tracks in the snow on their way home.

In other words, it was the kind of party Matt would've loved to be single at, so he was doubly or triply unhappy, for not only was he married, but the evidence of that—Jean—was by his side. Matt had his hand on my shoulder and was pulling me back a little, as if he was physically going to drag me off. He was four years older than me. Married young, too young, he seemed a little cranky about me hitting on Sam's friend. Or maybe it was the two hours' drive he had to make back to the Mount. He was still a little gun-shy after falling asleep at the wheel on 46 last month and waking up in a frozen, rutted cornfield without a muffler. I shrugged off his hand.

It was the crucial moment. The pot full of vegetarian chili on the stove was starting to burn on the bottom. Robin had red, frizzy hair that hid her ironic smile when she turned to the side. "Stay," she said, barely above a whisper. Matt turned me around. He was a big, strong dude—getting his master's in exercise. Central was the kind of school that gave out degrees in exercise. I myself had aced a bowling class. But it wasn't like high school and Outdoor Chef—that A wouldn't be enough to keep me in college.

"What the hell you doing, Red?" Matt asked. "I'm not driving back here tomorrow to get you."

"I know. . . . I'll hitch or something. Look at her hair. She's my long-lost sister," I said. "We're destined to have an incestuous relationship."

"You're a sick puppy," Matt said, shaking his head. I looked for Sam, but he was off in a corner of the kitchen explaining how to roll a joint to a doe-eyed coed from Ferris.

Jean was smiling—a little meanly, it seemed—and shaking her head at me. "C'mon, Matt. Red can screw this up all by himself."

I turned to Robin. "See how much confidence my friends have in me?"

What she saw in me, I wasn't sure—she was lonely and bored, sad and drunk. Everybody knows how to add up those numbers. She wanted me to stay, and that was good enough for me. I slithered away from Matt and stood in front of her against the kitchen counter, as if I was protecting her from something.

"I'm going to stay and have some more chili," I said.

I had a dog named Bruce that I was constantly neglecting. Matt would have to deal with a hyper Bruce when they got back. Bruce had taken to chewing up books and articles of clothing when the house was empty for long periods of time, so there was no telling what they'd find on West Center Street.

Earlier that year, I'd gone out with two Kims at the same time for three months. I had wanted to believe that those months were some of the best of my young life, though I was miserable the whole time. The truth is that the two Kims nearly destroyed me. I couldn't be responsible enough to feed my dog, so what was I doing sleeping with two girls named Kim? I wasn't helping my GPA, that's for sure. I'd been getting by on my good looks since eighth grade, and it seemed like I was stuck back there at age thirteen: if I could sleep with one girl, why not two? Matt was amused. "At least you can't goof up and call them by the wrong names," he said. Who was I trying to impress? I asked myself finally. Myself, I guess—some idea of myself I had invented, imagined to be desirable. Nobody but the Kims cared, and I'm not sure how much *they* actually cared, for when I broke it off with both of them, neither of them seemed to mind. We still talked to each other at parties. "How could we be so stupid?" they both told me once, laughing. It seemed like I had a short shelf life—beyond the looks, what did I have? Who did I want to be besides somebody who had a lot of sex and got bad grades?

■ ■ ■

Robin had little blinking Christmas lights strung everywhere. All the plants in her cold apartment were dying, but she sure had a lot of them. People were dancing in her sparsely furnished apartment to music "from the sixties, seventies, and eighties." Just like the slogan of the only semidecent radio station between Lansing and Grand Rapids. Out of despair, I had even started to listen to jazz. The public radio station out of Central aired "Night Side," an all-night jazz show. The night side was my side of the day, and whether I was drinking, having sex, or even studying, it was usually on the other side of midnight. I'd never been one for instrumental music, for anything without a hook, but I was beginning to like the endless drift of the cool jazz on "Night Side." I was getting ready to—to what?—to drift, I hoped. To close my eyes and float off on a raft to a new shore where everybody welcomed me gladly. Where I didn't have to concentrate to remember anybody's name. Where my own name would finally be enough, and I wouldn't have to pretend. Jazz. Cool jazz in an endless stream.

Robin didn't feel like she could abandon her own party, so we had to get drunker while waiting for everyone to clear out. I had my hand in her back pocket, and her tiny hand was up under my shirt, hanging on my hip at the top of my jeans. Her skin against mine, even that tiny fraction of skin, kept me from moving. The absence of that warmth whenever she moved to change the music or get another drink stung like an icy bee. Finally, she pulled Sam aside, and he agreed to stay and nudge the remaining stragglers home and pull the door closed while Robin and I got better acquainted.

■ ■ ■

We slipped into her bedroom, deposited the remaining coats in a pile outside the door, then went at it. Her bedroom had a mattress on the floor, a laundry basket, and random clothes strewn everywhere. Just like my room back in Mount P. I had high hopes, but that's all they turned out to be—*high* hopes. In a tangle and a flurry, we were naked, and after a quick, frenzied collision, I was done. And while I sought to apologize and to please her by other means—well, the one-night things; occasionally, there'd be some primitive ecstatic linkage that overcame awkwardness and unfamiliarity and even drunkenness, but usually, nobody had a clue what the other person wanted, and if you stopped to talk about it, you'd just realize how ridiculous the whole thing was, so you plowed on, even though you wanted to say, *Not like that,* or *Here, not there,* or *Faster,* or *Slower,* or *Please stop,* or *Please don't stop* or even *I can't breathe,* you plowed on till it was over—she became impatient and frustrated. She called me a boy, then went ahead and pleased herself. Good for her, I can say now, though then, as she turned away, as I desperately spooned against her and we drifted off, I felt desperately lonely. I imagined the car back on 46, and Jean with her foot out the door, trying to scrape through to pavement while I was sliding on ice into a sad, fitful sleep.

■ ■ ■

In the morning, the tiny white lights on her tiny blue Christmas tree continued to twinkle, as they had all night. On the mattress on the floor, I looked over at Robin, and she looked away and groaned. I reached toward her, but she gently kept me at arm's length.

She seemed torn between getting rid of me as soon as possible and simply trying to pretend I didn't exist. That was hard to do in that tiny apartment among the stale wreckage of the party. Outside, it was one of those gray Michigan days in December that made you feel like your laundry needed to be whiter. That maybe you shouldn't jam so much into the machines at the Laundromat. That maybe you should separate them into piles of color like your mother always told you to.

Her breasts were small and perfect. Her panties snug against her ass. I wanted her again, and even more. I wanted her sober and quiet. I wanted her and me against the gray weight pressing through the window. I tried to pull her to me, but she disappeared into a flurry of blankets.

"Let's not and say we did," she said semisweetly—I didn't know her well enough to read her level of sarcasm. "I don't feel so good," she said. She got up and stumbled to the bathroom, her bare feet thumping on the scarred hardwood floor.

■ ■ ■

She took a shower while I rummaged through the open shelves of her tiny kitchen. I spotted a coffee maker but could not find coffee. Finally, I boiled water and made myself a cup of Red Rose tea. I felt a desperate need to be happy, stupidly jaunty and upbeat.

She emerged from the bathroom in a ragged blue towel. "Hey, do you remember those old TV commercials for Red Rose tea, with monkeys dressed in clothes singing 'Red Rose Tea, Red Rose Tea'?" I began to dance around like a monkey, wagging my head and singing the jingle in my off-key hungover rasp.

"Uh, no, I don't. I don't—excuse me—even remember your name." She flushed a bit, then turned away from me to quickly pull on jeans and a wrinkled T-shirt from a bluegrass festival in Remus, Michigan, I myself had attended the previous spring. And I would've said something about that to her, but she didn't even remember my name.

"Red," I said angrily, pointing to my hair. "Tim."

"And I am?" she asked.

"Is this a test? You're Robin. I never got your last name, but you're Robin."

Big Rapids was surrounded by cornfields. Every city in that part of the state was a tiny island amid the wild seas of cornfields. In December, frozen, snow-covered cornfields. Robin was marooned in Big Rapids with a bunch of second graders. Sam was her friend, and, knowing Sam, that meant he'd slept with her at some point.

"Tim. Okay, how are you getting back to Mount Pleasant? I don't have a car."

"At least you remember where I'm from."

"Tim, don't go getting funny on me now. "

"Last night, you weren't so concerned about that," I said, pouting. "I can hitch or something, I guess."

"Sunday morning on 46? You'd be better off walking. I'll call Sam."

Sam. Yes, Sam would think of something. My head throbbed, and my belly ached and swirled from beer and chili. "You don't have any coffee?"

"I quit caffeine. I'll do anything to help me sleep. I watched you sleep last night."

Robin—the early bird. The state bird. Red bird. Red breast. She flitted around the tiny apartment in the stale, tense air. I felt like the loan of her space was rapidly coming due. She was a librarian who'd helped me find a book but now had other work to do.

Sam wasn't home. Or wasn't answering.

She made another phone call. I made another cup of tea. She

had three eggs in her fridge. I held them up, and she waved at me as if to say, *Whatever.*

"Mary Jean?" I heard her above the eggs' sizzle. "Yeah. I'm in a situation here. Yeah." Robin sounded both irritated and embarrassed. She crouched around the phone like it was a tiny fire she was nurturing to keep from freezing. "One of *those* situations. . . . Could you drive me and this guy over to Mount Pleasant this morning? Yes, a new *friend.* He lives in Mount Pleasant. . . . His friends left him here. Friends from Mount Pleasant. . . . My friend Sam's friends. . . . Sam's not home. . . . I don't know. . . . I'll pay for gas . . . and I'll buy you lunch."

I fried the eggs in one large, runny mass. The smell, which I usually loved, made me even more queasy. I'd never had a one-night stand where I was stuck like that, quickly and clearly and obviously a burden. My ears were burning. I took turns pressing them against the frosted window to cool them off.

■　■　■

"Mary Jean's gay, by the way," she said to me after she hung up. "If you offend her, we're going to abandon you in the middle of Roscommon County." Roscommon County was known as the home of the Michigan Militia, crazy old white guys with multiple tattoos and ridiculous amounts of firearms.

"Hey, I'm not going to look a gift lesbian in the mouth," I said.

"See, you're an asshole. I knew it," she said tersely, turning away from me.

"Why are you trying to make me feel like such a loser? Are you punishing me for something? You don't know me well enough to treat me like this," I said. It hurt my head to try to decipher my own logic.

"Red Rose, Red Rose Tea," she sang shrilly.

When Mary Jean pulled up, we stepped out from beneath the

torn "Powder Puff" awning and into the improbable Sunday morning sunshine. Robin shaded her eyes and looked up. I turned away
to study the abandoned storefront—the Powder Puff, a lingerie store
victimized by Wal-Mart like everything else. Even Kmart was losing out to Wal-Mart as they duked it out from either side of the
abandoned, seedy downtown. The "Clearance" sign was stenciled
onto a large sheet of paper—that, in itself, a throwback to earlier
times. The Scotch tape holding the sign to the smeared, dusty glass
was yellowing, peeling. I cupped my hands to the glass and peered
inside. A few loose, flimsy items were stacked on a table, pairs of
underwear too—too something—to find a home at even 75 percent
off. Wire hangers were strewn over the counter, and the spot where
the cash register must have sat was brighter, less discolored.

Mary Jean's horn made me jump.

"Hey," I said. I climbed into her backseat, the eggs jostling in
my gut. Robin was already sitting up front. I had long legs and was
usually offered the front. I turned and stretched them across the
backseat.

"Watch your boots back there," Robin said, though she was
looking at Mary Jean, not at me.

The truth was that I never watched my boots. I was not a boot
watcher. I usually got the floor muddy, then apologized later.

"Sorry," I said.

"Yeah, right," Mary Jean grunted. She smiled warily at Robin.
Two hours to Mount P. She had the radio tuned to a gospel station
from Mars. Or perhaps Chicago. When the winds blew right, you
could pick up stations from across the Midwest.

Mary Jean was clearly unhappy with me. Not for me, with me.
For sleeping with her friend. For dragging her out to drive four
hours across the flat palm of mid-Michigan because she had a car
and Robin didn't. Because she was in love with Robin. If she'd
known the particulars, perhaps she would have been grateful—if

Robin had any leanings in the other direction, the night with me had surely put them at a more extreme angle.

Mary Jean was interested in me as a specimen. A macho Detroit boy, a foreigner to the flat meat of Michigan's palm. I have always looked like a *guy* guy, and that's one reason that I've never had any trouble meeting women. I was a weight lifter, which is how I'd gotten tight with Matt. I was also pretty hairy. I was elected class president in ninth grade mainly due to the fact that I was able to grow a respectable mustache at that young age, though that was the beginning and end of my political career.

■　■　■

Mary Jean was tall and thin. When she sat up, her blond hair nearly brushed the ceiling in her old green Volvo. Where did one get a Volvo in Big Rapids? She had the look of a defeated athlete, hunched over the steering wheel as if she were afraid to extend her body to its natural proportions.

"How did Blue Jeans Day go?" Mary Jean asked abruptly. They'd had Blue Jeans Day at Central a couple of weeks earlier. The idea was that you were supposed to wear jeans if you supported gay rights.

"That was stupid," I said. "Everyone already wears jeans every day. That's like cheating or something. . . . So I guess it was a big hit. Everybody wore jeans—like usual."

"It's not cheating," Mary Jean said. "It forces you to go out of your way to say you *don't* support gay rights, and that's how it should be. People wear jeans every day, and everybody deals with gay people every day, even though they may not realize it. The point is that it's as ordinary as wearing jeans."

"No, no," I protested. "It's like stuffing the ballot box." We were all wearing jeans at that very moment. Robin sighed loudly enough to be heard over the hand-clapping gospel.

"Sometimes the ballot box needs stuffing," Mary Jean said. "Just to wake people up. You can unstuff the box once you get their attention."

"Didn't Ferris have Blue Jeans Day?" I asked.

"Everybody in Big Rapids is in the closet except for me and two dykes who run a janitorial service."

"Is that the name of it, Two Dykes Janitorial Service?"

Mary Jean snorted. "Oh, I like that. I really like that."

Robin, who was doing her best to ignore us, suddenly spoke up. "What about Rod and Jack down at the Landing?"

"Yeah, okay. Them, too. You just thought of them because you've got a crush on Rod."

Robin pressed her forehead into the cold window again and sank back into silence.

"We're living in the Snow Belt, but I call it the No Belt. No to anything that isn't considered normal. And they've got a pretty narrow slice of pie they call normal up here."

"You look normal," I said stupidly.

"Oh, thank you—you're too kind." She laughed again. I was beginning to like her. She'd grown up in Big Rapids and explained to me the M-46 landscape—the cultural landscape. Who went to Ferris, versus who went to Central, versus who didn't go to college at all, farmers versus shop rats, she had it all down. I, in turn, explained the racial landscape of Detroit, for Big Rapids also had very few blacks. "There's nobody in a closet in Detroit. That's where we hide the dead bodies," I said.

"So why'd she sleep with you, when she won't sleep with me?" Mary Jean asked out of the blue. Despite her show of reluctance, she seemed pleased to have Robin trapped in this way for the long car trip. The salted snow had melted to slush, and nobody had to drag a foot out the door, so we were making pretty good time.

I could think of no clever rejoinder, and besides, it looked as though Robin's head would explode through the window if she pressed against it any harder. When she turned to light a cigarette, her forehead was red with cold and pressure. The question hung in the air unanswered till it grew stale and settled to the floor like old smoke.

I think Mary Jean loved Robin because Robin was from someplace else and knew lots of lesbians. Though Robin wasn't a lesbian, despite Mary Jean's recruitment efforts, she didn't mind having one for a friend. She didn't mind being seen buying groceries at the Big Rapids IGA with one. Mary Jean's mother had disowned her until her infirmities triumphed over her stubborn disapproval, so Mary Jean currently lived at home and cared for her mother in the American tradition of the maiden aunt.

If she'd been at the party, Mary Jean could have formed an alliance of exclusion with the Glumbergs—all that heterosexual groping, and not one sign of any same-sex activity or potential. Mary Jean worked the night shift at the Big Rapids Nursing Home, so she was often exhausted. It was a small enough town to only have one nursing home. Grand Rapids was the big city. Big Rapids was Hicksville. Big Rapids was one high school and one high school only: Big Rapids High School. It had nearly crushed the only known lesbian in the school, Mary Jean. There's a big difference between Big and Grand, and she explained it to me in great detail.

■ ■ ■

You can learn a lot in a car with two strangers driving across the flat palm of Michigan. Or you can learn nothing at all.

"What are you majoring in?" Mary Jean asked. Last night, I'd given Robin my standard answer: "A good time." That or "Bowling." I was beginning to realize that it didn't take much education to mock education.

"Undeclared," I said.

"What year are you? Shouldn't you be declared by now?"

"I've deferred declaring," I said, thinking that sounded official.

"That could be a problem later on," Mary Jean said.

"It's a problem now," I said.

Robin seemed incredibly focused on the white nothing out her window. A lot of people don't realize that parts of Michigan are very similar to Ohio—it's our dirty little secret. We brag about all the lakes, but the center of the mitten's palm is a vast wasteland of flat cornfields and Michigan Militia training camps.

The vanity license plate on the car in front of us said "BIN-GOOOO."

"If I ever get that excited about bingo, I hope somebody shoots me," I said.

"What makes you so superior?" Mary Jean asked. "Bingo's harmless enough. There are worse things to be addicted to."

"Like what?" I asked.

"Drugs and alcohol," she answered.

I thought drugs and alcohol were necessary accessories for a good time.

"Sex," Robin mumbled.

"What?" Mary Jean and I both said.

"Yeah, sex. I mean, how long does it last? Usually, not very. I mean, a good buzz usually lasts longer, and as long as you're not driving, a lot safer. . . . Look at us right now. We're driving halfway across the fucking state . . ."

"*I'm* driving halfway across the fucking state. You're just admiring the scenery."

I waited for Robin to finish, but she didn't, and I suppose she didn't need to. I was the price she was paying for the brief blurry minutes of lust last night.

■ ■ ■

It would be my last semester at Central. I suppose I could've tried Northern or Eastern or Western. There was no Southern Michigan U. It was the U part that was the trouble. I went home for the holidays, and I never returned to Mount Pleasant. When I arrived back in Detroit with my tail between my legs—well, I'm not sure I was even mature enough to have a tail, though what I did have between my legs had gotten me . . . not very far—after having exhausted my father's patience and the money he'd saved for my college education, he got his revenge by quickly calling in a favor and getting me a job in the Chrysler plant he'd worked at since high school, interrupted only by his military service after Korea and before Vietnam. That hadn't stopped him from getting a tattoo in the Philippines and rightly accusing me of being lazy and wasting his hard-earned money and saying *I* should join the Army to get some discipline.

I fled the factory after six months when I called in a favor of my own and got a job as a fireman for the city of Warren, where I have worked the last eight years. One year, I was featured in the firemen's beefcake calendar they used for fund-raising. Like a lot of the guys, I lift weights during the downtime between runs. I asked them to put "Mr. Pleasant" as my name, or nickname, but they didn't get it. The marketing firm that volunteered to put it together wasn't interested in some clever fireman—they were just interested in my body.

I finally got married last year. To a beautiful nurse named Amy. My hair is thinning, though people still call me Red. I had arthroscopic surgery on my elbow last year. Too much bowling, I guess. I saved a dog from a burning house and got my picture in the paper once. I don't think I'll ever have an occasion to go back to Mount Pleasant again, or to ride two hours just to go to a party.

My sister Renee turned out to be a lesbian, at least for a while. She met a woman while she was in the Navy, and that lasted a few years. She just had a baby with some guy last year, though she's not marrying him. My father jokes about how I turned out to be "the normal one" after all. Renee holding that baby looks pretty normal to me—the love just washes over me when I'm in the room with her and that child.

■ ■ ■

I got out of the car, but then poked my head back in. "Want to come in for a while? Rest or something before the ride back?"

"No. No, thanks," Mary Jean said. "I want to get home and watch 'Bowling for Dollars.' And I think Robin's going to bingo down at the fire hall." She winked at me.

I laughed. I knew she was right—"Bowling for Dollars" was on Sundays at three, Denny McDonough hosting.

I had been thinking about what to say to Robin, but we were at good-bye time, and I still didn't have a clue. Since she was a friend of Sam's, I might see her again someday and have another chance to make a fool out of myself. I bent to the passenger-side window and could see how she'd smudged it during the ride. It was like the windows of the Powder Puff—nothing for sale, nothing on display.

She rolled it down. I bent down to kiss her cheek. "I'm sorry," I whispered.

"That's okay," she said. "Live and learn."

"Learn and burn," I said.

I knew I needed to say one more thing. I held up my arm to Mary Jean and ran back around to the other side of the car. I motioned for her to roll down her window and bent down toward her.

"Don't go kissing *me* now, you jerk," she said, but she was smiling.

"Thanks a lot for doing this," I said. I wanted to will her into accepting my sincerity. I extended my hand through the half-open window, and she awkwardly reached out and took it.

"Was it worth it?" she whispered back. Her breath curled out into the cold air and disappeared. The exhaust billowed behind us as the engine chugged impatiently.

I closed my eyes and let my head sag onto my chest with the weight of being an unloved burden on a gloomy December day. My hands pressed against the icy roof of the car, and my legs spread. I had assumed the position.

Mary Jean turned to Robin. "We'd better get the hell out of here. I'm starting to like this guy." And with that, they drove off.

I guess I'd thought that if I made friends with Mary Jean, it would somehow make things all right. But *somehow* is a tricky word—like "I somehow forgot about class," or "I somehow failed that exam," or "I somehow forgot to wear a condom." I wanted to feel like less of a fool, but it was as clear as that long, straight road between Big Rapids and Mount Pleasant that nothing was going to change. That weekend prompted me to abandon college—you might think that means I see it in a negative light, but I never felt such a burden lifting as I did when I packed up my stuff two weeks later and disappeared from Mount Pleasant forever.

There was no Mr. Pleasant—maybe that was what Robin thought as they drove away, as they were rid of me. Me, I stood in the street full of the thick sadness of the slushy day. "Was it worth it?" I noticed that the back of Mary Jean's car was plastered with political messages across the bumper and up onto the rear of the car. That car must've been the only place in her life where she could say what she meant.

Was *it* worth *it?* I couldn't even begin to define my *its.* But then I was on my way to being a college dropout. But then I was on my way.

In the backyard, Bruce was chained up, snuffling in the wet snow. When he saw me coming, he ran toward me till he got yanked by the end of the chain, choking himself with anticipation. I reached down to pet him. He was wildly wagging his tail as if I was there to rescue him. Like so many others, fooled by appearances. I unchained him. I let him loose.

The Chippewa Lacrosse Trick

"In 1763, as part of Pontiac's Rebellion, a group of Chippewa staged a ball game outside the stockade to create a diversion and gain entrance to the post and then attacked and killed most of the British occupants."

Fort Michilimackinac was a tourist trap at the foot of the Mackinac Bridge. At one time, a fort had indeed stood on that spot, though the wood of the gate they now passed through was raw and unweathered. Everything had been "reconstructed" with the tourist trade in mind. Tom had visited the fort when he was a child, and now he was there with his wife, Julie, as part of their Michigan tour, a nostalgic trip to show her scenes from his childhood. His family had vacationed every summer in Michigan, circling the Great Lakes in their Apache camper.

"Jesus Christ."

Tom heard the startled voice behind him, and the fearful tone. He turned quickly. He knew who it was.

"Fran?" They stood frozen in front of the stockade. Julie tugged on his sleeve.

"Tom Forester," Fran said in a dark monotone. It'd been eight years. He turned away from her squint.

"Fran, this is my wife, Julie," he said quickly. "How are you? What are you doing here? Do you live around here?" The questions tumbled forth despite Tom's longing to hold back, play it cool. He paused. The women eyed each other warily.

Fran's hands gripped a double stroller with an infant and a toddler in it. She stood next to a muscular, stylishly dressed man who stared blankly at Tom.

"This is my husband, Martin, and my children, Heloise and Renee." She turned to her husband. "I went to college with him," she explained.

Tom shook hands formally with Martin. "Pleased to meet you." After graduating from Central Michigan University, Tom had moved from Mount Pleasant back home to Chicago. Fran had stayed at the college to help run the Paris exchange program. He'd seen her just one time since graduation.

The fort was at the tip of Michigan's mitten, perhaps the white rim at the end of a fingernail. Mount Pleasant was in the soft flesh at the center of the palm.

"What are you doing now? Still painting?" Tom asked. Fran looked pale and exhausted. He didn't think she was still painting.

"What are you doing?" she asked, ignoring his questions.

"Well, I didn't go to law school. I'm doing theater work," he said, and Julie gave him a look.

"That's a shame. You should have gone," Fran said. "You would've made a great lawyer." She'd always wanted him to stick with his interest in theater. Maybe she'd forgotten. He shuffled his feet in the pure white dust.

Tom had switched majors from prelaw to drama until his father found out and threatened to cut off funding. Tom didn't have enough money to pay his own way. He had no recourse but to switch back to prelaw. After graduation, he worked at a bank for five years, and then, on a whim, he had auditioned for a theater troupe that performed on cruise ships. He was offered a part, so he quit the bank job and took off on the boat, where he met Julie.

The cruise ship was a lark, and after two years, they'd both had enough. They stepped off the boat with some vague idea that they should get serious about their future together, and ended up getting married. That'd been six months ago. In Chicago, Julie had been substitute teaching, while Tom was temping at American Red Cross. They were both trying out for amateur theater productions in the area, but as newcomers they weren't faring well with the cliquish local drama crowd.

"As you can see," Tom said, "I look the same. I've changed, though. In good ways, I think."

"Gray hair," Fran said. "Your hair was always so nice. And long. Have you seen pictures of him with long hair?" She turned to Julie.

"Yeah," Julie said. "He looked pretty wild." She gave Tom a questioning look. She knew little of his past, and old girlfriends were not part of the nostalgia tour. On the boat, the past was imaginary or nonexistent—you could talk about it, or lie about it. Tom had chosen silence and vagueness.

"Yes," Fran said, adjusting the stroller to provide more shade for her children. "Wild."

Tom's hair was prematurely gray, and he'd dyed it for the cruise ship revue. Once they quit, he let it grow out. Julie wanted him to go back to dyeing it, which surprised him. She seemed to want little artifice in their lives.

"It's like we're on the cruise ship all over again," Julie had said, "but now we're stuck without parts." She liked making analogies. She had a knack for it.

■ ■ ■

"Fran, I love you," Tom shouted into the pay phone. He was calling from a Big Boy restaurant right outside Mount Pleasant. He'd taken off work at noon and driven up from Chicago to surprise her. He was waiting for the right moment to tell her where he was.

"Where are you? I hear traffic," she said.

"I'm closer than you think," he told her, tired and almost giddy from the long drive full of anticipation. He hadn't seen her since graduation three months earlier, though he'd called her frequently.

"Not too close, I hope," she said.

"Maybe, maybe too close," he said. He was too tired to drive all the way back to Chicago. "I thought I might drive up and see you," he ventured.

"Where are you? Did you? Don't!" Tom heard the phone being fumbled, adjusted. He thought he heard whispering, but maybe it was the road, the connection, his own breathing. "You can't," she said, her voice breaking on "can't," then leveling out. "I've got plans."

They'd never agreed not to see others, but it was clear that neither of them had for the last six months of school. He had spent nearly every night in her apartment the last two or three of those months.

Tom hung up. He swung open the restaurant door, sat down at a booth, and ordered coffee. Coffee and a Big Boy combo, for he was suddenly hungry. He had room again, though he didn't want it. He'd wanted to close the gap, at least for a weekend—to be full and certain that she was still in his life.

■ ■ ■

"She still paints," Martin said. Tom felt ready to explode with fear and discomfort. And excitement, too. Their children were fussing in the stroller, but Fran let them fuss.

"Good," Tom said. "That's good. Hanging on to your dreams."

Tom looked at Julie as if to say, "Help me out here." Julie rolled her eyes. It was clear she preferred to stay silent and make jokes about it later.

"Did you just get here?" Tom asked. He'd been describing the family photo of him and his brother Jake in the stocks when he'd heard Fran's voice.

"Yes," Fran said. "We have to keep moving," she said, pointing to the children. "As if they were props," Julie would say later to comfort him, to try to squeeze out the wedge Fran had left between them. "She and Martin seemed like two overly serious puppets."

Tom remembered Fran spending hours combing out her long, black, shiny hair. She had a thin dancer's body and thick, full lips. She still looked great. He shuddered, remembering the last time he had touched her. The fort was small, and they'd be running into each other again, though they all pretended otherwise.

"Hey, could you take our picture in the stocks together?" Julie suddenly asked, her voice unnaturally high-pitched.

Fran looked at Martin. "No, no, sorry, I . . . I just can't." She shrugged and smiled, looking down again at her children.

"Well, nice meeting you, Fran and . . . Martin," Julie said cheerfully. "Beautiful children you have."

"Yes," Martin said. He seemed bored by the entire encounter, while Julie was clearly intrigued. Tom felt sure that Martin had never heard Fran mention him before. If she had, things might have taken a different turn.

"Great seeing you," Tom said.

"What a surprise," Fran said.

Tom and Julie walked away. He was dazed, light-headed. The fort seemed minuscule, and he didn't know what direction to go in to avoid Fran and her family. And he wasn't sure he wanted to.

"This really is a nostalgia tour," Julie said, squeezing his hand.

"Old flames everywhere. But I'm here to put out any fires." She squeezed harder.

"Let's sit down awhile," he said. "Let them get ahead of us."

"Oh, I think they already are," said Julie. "I just can't," she mimicked. "It's my painting finger. I don't want to damage it." Tom laughed and squeezed back, though he knew he hardly deserved whatever civility Fran had given him.

■ ■ ■

The big souvenir item in the area was Mackinac Island fudge, and Tom had bought a small box of it at a roadside stand that morning. From the fort's lookout, they could see the island out in Lake Michigan, distant, miragelike. He pulled the fudge out of his backpack and cut it with the little plastic knife that came in the box. "The locals around here call the tourists Fudgies," Tom said. He thought Julie might like that.

"You mean I came all this way just to be a Fudgie?" she said. "This is horrible, by the way." She dropped her half-eaten piece of fudge into a wooden fort trash receptacle.

"Didn't they burn all their trash back then?"

"Too sweet," Tom said. "I don't know how we ever ate it as kids." But he kept eating.

"It must taste better on the island," Julie said. "I got a sense you two were pretty serious. I don't remember you saying much about her."

"You know me, I'm not one of those guys who talks about his old girlfriends all the time," Tom said in a self-congratulatory way, though it was true. He tended to connect them with old versions of himself that he had discarded. He had willfully tried to discard as much of Fran as he could.

"Spare me the details," Julie said.

"I have," he said. "I have."

Six months—it seemed like a long time back then. The pressure of graduation made it that much more intense—how close would they get before it was time for him to take his diploma and leave? Some couples at school were getting engaged. Others were splitting up under the weight of the looming choices.

■ ■ ■

After eating his combo and drinking three cups of coffee, he should have understood, should have simply driven home. But he wanted to hold her, needed to. The coffee just intensified his frenzy. Should he call again? He thought of that long black hair falling against his chest as they made love. He could not bear it. If this was the end, he wanted to at least see her one last time. He had come all that way.

He drove quickly to her apartment near campus. A light on in the kitchen. He got out and ran up the drive. He could barely breathe. He pounded on the door.

She opened it quickly, but just a crack. "Pizza man," he said, though the tone was all wrong—defiant, angry. It was what he'd planned on saying initially, as a joke, before he'd chickened out and called first.

She opened the door wider. "You didn't, you didn't drive up all the way up here? Tom Forester, you are crazy." She smiled a half-smile and shook her head.

"Were you expecting some other Tom?" he asked.

"Oh, come on in," she said, exasperated. "Alan's over. You remember Alan from the mime troupe."

So, it was Alan, Tom thought—or was it? Was there anyone? Alan was a wimpy scarecrow, meek and accommodating, only a junior. Tom moved forward to embrace and kiss her, as he'd planned, even with Alan there, but she was already turning back into the kitchen. She was treating him like a neighbor stopping by, not a lover she hadn't seen in three months. Tom balled his fists and followed her.

■ ■ ■

At eleven every morning, they shot off a cannon from outside the fort along the Lake Michigan shore.

"How come it's MackiNAW Island but Fort MichilimackiNACK?" Julie asked. They stood waiting in the large crowd. It was hot and dusty, a dry summer for Michigan. The lake looked wonderfully blue and pure and untouchable.

Tom had a habit of not answering questions he didn't know the answers to, so it hung in the air. He was searching the crowd for Fran—a cannon blast from the past.

"The cannon will probably scare the shit out of those babies," Julie said. "If they're out here."

With Julie, he had always, always been gentle, so gentle she had asked him once if he was even attracted to her sexually—his gentleness mistaken for disinterest. Tom was a big man. He worked out in a gym, pushing himself till every muscle ached.

The cannon blast rang out suddenly with a jolt, echoing over the water. Then, as the smoke lingered in the air, the men in colonial uniforms marched solemnly away. The show was over, and the crowd was quickly dispersing.

"Boom," Julie said as they stood waiting for something else to happen. It was almost lunchtime, and they had probably seen enough of the fort. They were taking a midafternoon boat out to Mackinac Island, so they had some time to kill. He was looking forward to going on the boat, walking around the island where no cars were allowed, to have the world slowed down and controlled. Though what if Fran was going there, too?

Tom had written and apologized to Fran after what happened on that trip back to Mount Pleasant, and she'd written him back to accept his apology. Seeing her again made the shame and guilt fresh and raw, as if he'd been scalped by his old sins. He desperately wanted to bump into her again and say something else, though he wasn't sure what. "I'm sorry *again?*" "*Still?*" "I'm *more* sorry?" Would it matter to her at all?

They walked back inside the wooden walls. What Tom remembered most about the fort was a large model of the "Chippewa Lacrosse Trick." Once, a group of Indians playing lacrosse outside the fort's walls had deliberately thrown the ball over the fence. When the trusting soldiers opened the gate to let them retrieve it, the Indians attacked and took the fort. He'd wanted to arrange the figures to prevent the bloodshed that was coming, but the figures were under glass, unreachable.

He couldn't find the model anywhere. He'd told Julie about it on the drive up. He remembered that the tiny Indians had frightened and fascinated him. Tom wanted to see it again, to look at their faces once more. How trusting were the soldiers? Were the Indians portrayed as evil caricatures, savages, fierce and devious? What was the tone of the display? Had they changed it to make it more politically correct? He wanted to look at the face of the soldier opening the gate to let them in.

Tom finally found a guide and asked him. He said they'd taken it down long ago because it was historically inaccurate.

"What's the true story, then?" Tom asked.

"It's complicated," the guide said. He was leading a tour group of retirees through the fort, and Tom had interrupted him.

"A lot of people ask about that model," he said, and continued with the tour, leaving Tom and Julie standing in the dust.

"Come on," Tom said. "Let's go get a rubber tomahawk or something."

"Is that the name of a drink?" Julie asked. "Because I could use one."

Tom walked toward the gift shop, his feet dragging in the dust. He was trying to remember after so many years of trying not to: how hard had he pushed? He wanted to talk about it—with Julie, not Fran. The woman he loved and confided in. But she wouldn't be able to answer. How hard?

■ ■ ■

"Hi, Alan," he said. "You still miming?" Tom had always considered mimes as drama wannabes whose only skill was exaggeration. He thought they trivialized what he'd been forced to give up. The school had a mime troupe taught by a young French professor who'd gotten Fran interested. He was the real threat, Tom had always thought. He surveyed the room for the whiff of sex, some telltale sign of it, but noticed nothing. Though she had plans with Alan, some kind of plans.

"Hi, Tom. I thought you graduated," Alan said smugly.

"Nah, I came back for some remedial work with Fran here."

"Well, I think she's booked up at the moment," Alan said dismissively. It wasn't the Alan Tom remembered—he seemed more confident, at home there in Fran's apartment.

Tom circled the room, then quickly lunged at the kitchen table where Alan sat. Fran tried to work her way in between them, pushing Tom back. Tom didn't think Alan would fight. "Why don't you get out of here? I've got to talk to Fran. I just drove eight hours nonstop to be with her. I don't have time to chitchat with you."

Tom had never been one to get into fights. He thought of himself as a gentle, thoughtful person. Someone in control. But all that seemed like artifice now, a convenient pose.

"Isn't it more like five hours, Tom? I don't think it's your place to say who leaves and who stays," Alan said, pulling his feet up into the lotus position like he was staying forever, meditating himself into a stubborn bliss.

Fran had been oddly quiet. Tom thought she must be enjoy-
ing their posturing, knowing she was the one with the real power.
He suddenly felt something surging through him, some malignant
energy kicking in that he could not control. He lunged past Fran
and grabbed Alan by the throat, knocked him to the floor.

"Leave him alone!" Fran screamed. "Just grow up, will you?
Who do you think you are, barging in like this?" Tom backed away,
though the surge was still rising.

"Alan, maybe you'd better leave," Fran said, helping him up.
"I'll take care of this. I'll call you later," she said loudly, for Tom's
benefit.

"Are you sure you're going to be okay?" Alan asked as she led
him to the door.

"Yes, I'll be fine," she said confidently.

■ ■ ■

Julie and Tom browsed in the souvenir shop, making fun of whatever they could. The snow globe with the fort in it, the wolverine
salt and pepper shakers. More fudge. Saltwater taffy. "They must
import the saltwater," Julie said, trying to get him back from his
silence and distraction. The emptiness created by what he hadn't
told her lingered in the sweet, stuffy, potpourried air.

They wedged themselves down the tight aisles of the tiny shop,
careful not to knock anything off the closely packed shelves. Tom
bought a postcard of the fort to send to his brother. Julie bought an
oven mitt in the shape of Michigan.

The wolverine was the state animal, though there were no
wolverines in Michigan. "What's the difference between a lie and
a myth?" he asked.

She grabbed his hand as they exited the shop.

"A myth lasts longer," he said, answering himself.

"You think so?" She took her hand back.

The sun's glare reflected off their car in the gravel parking lot. Tom squinted, then lowered his head. He'd nearly given up on spotting Fran again, but just as he unlocked the car door, he spotted them farther down the parking lot, close to the exit gate, piling into an oversized van.

"Hey," Tom yelled, and waved. Fran and Martin looked up, paused, then continued loading up their van. They were too far away for Tom to walk up to them—or worse, run—without seeming strange and awkward. It would have to be to say something important. They were putting their kids in car seats. Tom's stomach roiled with cheap fudge. Julie sat in the hot car, glaring up at him as he watched the van pull away.

■ ■ ■

After Alan left, Fran rushed toward him and flew into angry tears.

"What the hell are you doing here?" she cried.

"I love you!" he cried back. "I needed to see you."

"What in the world possessed you to just—just *show up?*" She beat on his chest with her fists. "You're such a fucking asshole," she said, and she usually didn't talk that way.

"I wanted to be impulsive. You always told me I needed to be looser, less in control." That much was true. She had often told him to take off his imaginary tie.

She fell back against the wall with an agonized sigh.

"I want you to apologize to Alan," she said. "There was no need for that. That was a high school stunt."

She was patronizing him. Tom wanted to ask her what the deal was with Alan. He wanted to be reassured. But that would be "high school," too. He wanted to hold her. He wanted to be kissed. He did not want to apologize. She had allowed him to stay. She was in control. He wanted to change all that. He was still breathing heavily. He could not slow down. He could not speak. He rushed over to her and pulled her into his arms. He began kissing her. She turned her face away from him. He tried to push his hands between her legs, but she resisted. She was wearing tight black jeans and a black turtleneck.

"No," she said. "Not this. Not now. We have to sit down and talk."

He said, "Yes, this. Yes, now." He yanked her jeans open, pulling her zipper down quickly, and shoved a hand down between her legs, lifting her shirt with the other hand. She was frantically clawing at him. He leaned on her, and they fell over onto the couch. She was squirming and bucking violently. He would not hurt her, but he did not know how to stop, how to back away. The power surge was winding down. The sprint toward madness was over. She was yanking his hair, and he winced in pain, but he wanted to pull away by himself, to not be forced, to let her know he was giving up voluntarily. He tried to slowly rise away from her, but she got a good kick in as he did.

What could he say now? Was that him losing inhibitions, was that where letting go led? What other mad things lay just beneath the surface? He knew he had to leave.

"I'm sorry, I love you," he blurted out, and rushed to the door.

Fran was screaming, "Get out, now!"

He could not sleep. He drove through the night, then did not sleep through the next day, locked inside his room, trying to get himself back, back enough to see things clearly, to find the point where he'd gone into free fall. To erase that point. Finally, he collapsed and slept for twelve hours. His parents were away on vacation. He could not bring himself to call Fran. He wrote a whole series of letters that began with "I'm sorry. It wasn't me." The one he sent simply said, "I'm sorry." It was as far as he could go, the rest all blinding white space.

■ ■ ■

He knew he'd crossed a line, violated another person, violated his own idea of himself. He went back to his bank job and tried to imagine it never happened, but it stayed with him—a black regret that emerged at night in the catalogue of his nightmares. He'd never had to acknowledge or confront it in any public way again until today. That freedom had been a gift from Fran, and he knew now what he'd wanted to do. To acknowledge what she'd done for him with her silence, then, and again today—and it would take more than "Hey."

"You want me to tell you about her?" he asked Julie in the car. He had just spotted a Big Boy—they were all over Michigan. You could depend on them.

Julie stuck her hand out the window and said nothing for a long time. "Oh, I don't know," she said sadly.

"I will if you want," he said. "It's not pretty." He pulled into the Big Boy parking lot.

"Oh, well, if it's not pretty, I definitely don't want to know. . . . As long as you didn't rape her or something."

Tom reached between the seats for his sunglasses. He knew a response was called for. He flipped the switch and closed all the windows, then turned on the AC.

"That's a strange question," he said.

"It wasn't a question," she said. "You said it wasn't pretty."

"I didn't rape her, for Christ's sake."

They sat there in air-conditioned silence, watching the steady flow of summer weekend traffic whoosh past along the interstate.

"Being married isn't like going to confession," Julie said suddenly. "We don't need to know all of each other's sins, do we?"

"No," he said. "No. Some things I wish I remembered better.

Some things I want to forget, but I remember too clearly." His hand was in the fudge box. He couldn't stop.

"You should never trust your memory," Julie said. She was trying to help him, to convince him not to open the gate.

"The Indians fooled the soldiers," he said.

"They made the mistake of trusting," Julie said. "Why fight so much about the stupid fort? Why didn't everybody just build their own little fort and live in it and leave everybody else alone?" she blurted out.

They could see the answer from where they'd stood—the fort stood between Lake Huron and Lake Michigan on the Straits of Mackinac. Whoever controlled that strip controlled the lakes—who went from one lake to the next, who crossed over to the Upper Peninsula.

"We're all like Trojan horses," Tom said.

"Hey, I'm the poet in the family," Julie said.

"You are," he said. "I'm sorry." You open the gates out of curiosity, trust, anger, love—gates that should stay closed—and what happens?

He was sorry. There was nobody to call. He would eat his Big Boy combo this time and then simply love his wife as he should. It would be time to go to the boat docks soon. On the boat, they could entertain each other, just like on the cruise ships. He would dye his hair for her, he decided. He'd do whatever she asked.

Society of Friends

"They can't be Quakers," my wife, Verna, said. **"They're just renting** out the hall or something."

I didn't even know Detroit had a Quaker whatever-you-call-it. We were lost in a neighborhood drenched with decay and street-corner drug sales.

"Let's see what they're selling. Pick up something for the road," I said.

"Yeah, that's how Dena got killed."

"Woman had no business cruising these streets alone. Besides, I was just kidding." I turned up my wrists to show her my clean arms.

"Fuckin' Dena," she said. "Now Kathy marrying this married dude. What the hell's happening to my friends?"

"They're growing up?"

"They're committing suicide, that's what."

"He ain't married no more, is he?"

"Nah, it's the Mormons that can have more than one. His wife—ex—is ready to slit Kathy's throat."

"That's what Mormons do. They don't believe in guns."

"You're fucked up, you know that? He's got a kid nearly as old as Kath—a pothead, I hear."

"Hey, Ma, wanna get stoned?"

Verna punched me hard in the shoulder. Verna Gold. Kept her own name. Been married three times before. Gold's the second dude's name—that's when she gave up on changing. My name's Dave Silver—no shit, though everybody just calls me Silver. Kathy thought we should hyphenate and get a dog named Copper. I kind of liked the idea of naming a kid Zinc, even without the Gold. Zinc Silver, crime buster. Zinc Silver, rock star memorabilia salesman. Zinc Silver, balloonist and thrill seeker.

"There—that's the street!"

I stopped and pulled a U in the middle of the rubble, almost hitting two little kids walking down the middle of the street like it was a sidewalk.

"Goddamn kids. You almost hit them."

We were swinging on the rusty hinge of the second half of our lives, with just enough strength to hold on ourselves.

"Yeah, we ain't having no kids." It was the first time I'd said it aloud. Verna gave me a look, then turned quickly back toward the window.

"What's she see in this bald dude?" I asked, reaching for her hand across the seat.

"Big dick." She snorted.

"You didn't have much luck . . ."

"I'm kidding, asshole. I don't know—maybe she likes to polish the fucking thing and tell the future with it. She was seeing him on the sly for so long, once she had the habit, even when it was legit, she never talked about him."

"Here it is." I pulled in front of what looked like an old elementary school. The city'd been closing them up as it lost population.

"These folks gotta go halfway across town to get groceries, now their kids gotta sit on the bus for an hour just to go to school. America, ya gotta love it."

"Do I?" Verna asked. We were both still amazed by how cruel our country could be, though we didn't do much about it anymore except to comment on it in passing.

We'd gotten married by the JOP in Steubenville, Ohio, and had our picture taken in front of the mural of Dean Martin. Dino. "Everybody Loves Somebody Sometime" . . . "That's Amore." Two years ago, and we'd been happy ever since, to the amazement of all who knew us. When I was growing up there, they called it Stupidville. *We* called it Stupidville. Now it's the City of Murals. Everybody's gotta have a gimmick sometime . . .

An old hippie in a battered gray Volvo beeped his horn at us and waved as he passed. I had no idea who it was, but I waved back on principle. Kathy was marrying her teacher from dental hygienist school. She was gonna be rolling in the dough now. She'd never have to buy floss again.

Kathy's first husband was my brother, Luke, who didn't have a penny to his name, then or now. Lasted all of six months. Luke had lived in a homeless shelter for much of the winter and was now back on the street. Kathy and I shared Luke—the guilt and anger, the helplessness and failure, and the fact that either of us could've ended up there with him.

We got out of the car, a sand-colored Escort I bought when I thought I was going to live on the beach forever. Rusting out on the bottom. Looks like somebody's rotten tooth.

■ ■ ■

Damn it, they were Quakers, all right. The Society of Friends, they called the place. We walked into this big room full of uncomfortable benches and plopped down on one of them. I spotted who must've been the pothead son sitting sullenly at the end of the front row, and Kathy's parents, bewildered in their fancy clothes. Verna waved them over to join us. Nothing had started yet—everybody walking in and sitting quietly. Perry the master hygienist was sitting across from Kathy in large facing chairs in the middle of the room.

"Is this where we get to throw stones?" I whispered to Verna. She hit me again.

Kathy's parents had gotten up and were moving back to join us, but Kathy stood up and pointed vigorously to the front row, near the pothead, like she was trying to discipline a disobedient pet. I nudged Verna, and she reluctantly led Kathy's parents back up front. "But we want to sit with you," I heard her mother whisper loudly. Verna shrugged and patted her on the back. I watch Verna's nice ass swaying up to the front. She always had a nice ass. I could watch her walk to the fucking moon and not get tired of it. I cracked my knuckles. She was back in a flash.

"Shouldn't Friends get to sit wherever they want?" I asked. "The Society of Friends . . . isn't that . . ."

Verna cut me off. "Listen, asshole. My best friend's getting married. Let's not be Mr. Cynic here."

I caught the pothead's eye and winked at him. He didn't know who I was, but to him we all must've been unindicted co-conspirators. He shot me with his finger. Were we mocking each other out? It was hard to tell. I put my fingers to my lips and inhaled a mock joint. He laughed, and I could hear his father frown—it'd gotten that quiet.

The idea seemed to be that when the spirit moved them, they'd get up and marry each other, because Perry had to sit there ten more minutes just to get the spirit back after my exchange with Junior. Finally, they stood up and said their vows to each other—they wrote their own, though Kathy's sounded a little like old Fleetwood Mac lyrics.

"Tell it, girl!" Charlene, another old friend, shouted from behind us, thinking that's how it worked in the Society of Friends. She got a nervous laugh from nearly everybody.

After they sat down, I stood up to leave, and so did Kathy's folks, but everybody else stayed in their seats. Kathy waved us back like she was bringing down a helicopter. All her gestures seemed exaggerated in that toned-down setting. Kathy always needed a room with noise—she fed off noise. I shrugged and fell back onto the hard bench.

"Quaker Oats," I mumbled under my breath.

If you felt inspired, you were supposed to get up and say something nice about the bride and groom. I guessed it'd be bad for somebody to just jump up and speak. You had to wait awhile, think some deep thoughts. People had to go deep to get some good thoughts for this one. I don't know how Kathy got her parents to even show up. Her mother looked doped up pretty heavy, leaning against her husband like it was a funeral.

■ ■ ■

Rehab was a joke, but a joke I had to take seriously after laughing it off the first couple of times. I was never much of a talker, but they wanted you to talk about everything, and all the time. I just wanted to crawl inside myself for a while and lick my big wound until I could open my eyes and see straight. But it took a long time to climb back up after ten years stumbling down that dizzy staircase.

Verna and I were both addicted to the idea of happiness. This perfect happiness that didn't allow for downtime. Since there's no such thing as perfect, neither of us was doing very well when we met. She married me two years after her third divorce, six months after I'd gotten clean. It'd been my third trip to rehab, so we had this kind of synchronicity going with threes.

"Verna, why don't we take it one day at a time?" I say to her whenever I want to get a laugh. Now, I couldn't *stop* talking.

Both addiction and rehab were full of rituals, so I'd grown to associate them with failure, but here, they were defiantly absent of ritual, and what was left was only discomfort. Boy, this reception's going to be a real riot, I was thinking, sitting there staring at my hands.

The last time I'd been in any kind of church was when I went to a Serbian Orthodox baptism for my sister Lil's kid. Lil and her husband had to spit the devil out as part of the ceremony. I think I'd have a damn coughing fit trying to get the devil out of me. Kathy is one good-looking woman, so in a way, I don't blame the bald guy. I can see the temptation. Teenage boys drive their parents to extremes. His ex-wife put on some pounds due to stress. I've bailed out of a responsible life so many times, I shouldn't be judging anybody.

We got them a gift certificate to Chi-Chi's for a wedding present. I work there, back in the kitchen. I've been cooking in restaurants for fifteen years. Not good ones, mind you. Chains, mostly. Not fast-food takeout but sit-down chains. They don't mind the gaps in my employment record so much. Verna makes pretty good money as a manager at a catering company.

She mentioned hiring me once. "We don't want to go there," I said.

"Well, don't go getting unemployed on me, big boy," she said with a dark look. "Idleness is the devil's backseat."

"What?" I said.

"Whatever," she said.

I think she meant I might end up going for the four-bagger in terms of rehab. I love the name Verna. She's the only Verna I've ever met. The only Verna for me.

■ ■ ■

Okay, damn it, here's what I did. It seemed like we'd been there for hours. Maybe it *had* been hours—not a clock in the place. More than half the people in the room had spoken. People who had been sitting in long silence finally got up, only to say what somebody else had already said. Somebody mentioned the wine of forgiveness and the wine of love, and soon that was everybody's favorite comparison. Oh, yeah, they got jazzed on that one. In rehab, they would've shouted those people down. Me, Verna, the stoner boy, and her parents were among the holdouts. Then I cracked.

I began to stand. Verna tried to yank me back down. Have I said how strong she is? I think she could seriously kick my ass if it came down to it. But I pulled away. I saw Kathy—the only other one there who really knew me—put her face in her hands. Talk about messing with a dude's confidence.

The stoner perked up a bit. I'm one of those old hippies who's going bald with a ponytail. You know the type.

"Hey, everybody," I said. "I'm from the City of Murals, Steubenville, Ohio. Anybody seen the Dean Martin mural there? Anyway, my name is Silver, and I'm married to this beautiful woman to my left. I know Kathy pretty well, and she's a mighty fine lady, and I was just sitting here thinking this is the weirdest damn wedding I've ever been to. And I've been to some weird ones. Including my own." Verna kicked my shin extremely hard, and I jumped up and away from her. I hadn't been anywhere I had to watch my language in a long, long time, and I wasn't about to start now. In rehab, you could cuss a fluorescent blue streak, and no one would flinch. "I'm not sure what she sees in the old bald guy—Perry, excuse me—I'm losing it on top myself, so I feel I can say this—but I ain't heard nobody saying anything I haven't read on a wedding card. Not that I'm a great poet or nothing, but hey, if nobody's in charge, then let's get it on. It's like a school with no teacher. We can say what we think, right? Being married's hard shit—Verna here, the stories she could tell you . . ." I took a step away from her out into the aisle. "I ain't judging nobody, but hey, this one's kinda messy, so if the damn marriage is gonna work, I think people better get it all out in the open right now. Me, no matter what happens, Kath, you can clean my teeth forever. I've been through a lot of programs, and they're always trying to get everybody to talk. I don't want to mess things up, but I tell you who I'd like to hear from—Junior over there, and Kathy's folks. Who else would like to hear from them?" I looked around, and a few people were kind of half raising their hands, so I started doing a little rhythmic applause, and some people started clapping along, probably tired of being quiet for so long and trying to think deep thoughts. I'm kind of blessed with not having too many deep thoughts. It's like I put a layer of cement in there to keep me out of the basement.

After I got out of rehab the first time, I went to my grandmother's house asking for money to get a fix. You can't sink much lower than terrorizing your own grandmother, an easy mark living alone. Her hands shook as she handed me what she had. My hands were shaking, too. That's all I cared about—my hands. Heroin makes you believe you are the center of the universe. Everyone and everything else just falls away.

Surprisingly, the kid stood up pretty quickly, as if he'd been waiting to get called on. Everybody got quiet. "Man, this whole act sucks," he said. "It ain't fair to my ma. Just because she got a little fat."

Perry stands up then. "Jason, sit down. You don't know what you're talking about."

It looked as if he'd been ready to sit down anyway, but then it was like he stood up even taller. "Listen, Dad. Kathy's a babe and all, but man, you're old enough to have kids her age. Isn't that a little weird?"

Kathy stood up. "Yeah, yeah, it's a little weird. Love is weird, Jason."

"Amen to that!" Charlene shouted.

"I'll second that," somebody else said.

"Let's go have some cake," somebody else said.

"I'll drink to that," somebody else said.

"No drinks," somebody else said.

"No drinks? I thought this was the Friends Meeting House. Like a drinking club." It was becoming pretty clear who Kathy's friends were.

I could hear Charlene humming "Love Is Strange." I always loved that song. The Quakers among us were respectfully silent, or in shock. Some people rose to their feet to make a break for it, but then Kathy's father, Mitch, stood, and they sat down again.

Verna was squirming. "Look what you got started."

"Yeah, ain't it great?" I said, and winked at her.

"Speaking for Kathy's family," her father began, "you can all probably guess we're pretty uncomfortable with all this. The age thing, sure. The affair—Kathy, we're not idiots—we weren't sure we were going to come. I know I could use a drink about now, myself."

Some people laughed. I didn't. Dean Martin should've come back to Steubenville to die. He was lonely in Vegas.

"But here we are. Damn it, I hope it works, Kathy. And Mr. Rhodes, you mess with my daughter, I'll . . . well, just try to love her as much as we have. She's not easy to live with. You'll find that out soon enough." He got a few chuckles. I was starting to like the old dude. He didn't sound like the ogre Kathy and Luke had made him out to be.

Your mother . . . " he began again, looking down at his wife, a Chihuahua of a woman with big eyes darkly circled. "It's going to be hard. Don't expect any big hugs from us. The guy with the ponytail was right." He damn well knew my name, but I guess at the moment he didn't want to acknowledge that rickety bridge to Luke, and the past. I smiled at him anyway and raised my fist in a power salute, which he ignored. "I swore I'd never be the kind of guy who stopped talking to members of his own family. I'm not going to start now. So, well, good luck, you two. Let's all get out of here. I'm sweating like a pig."

"Amen," Charlene said again. We all applauded, then rose to our feet. Punch and cake were waiting out in the lobby.

Lousy punch, the kind with the ice cream in it to keep it cold, but the thing had gone on so long that the ice cream had melted the punch into this pinkish swamp algae. I guzzled five quick glasses, and Verna wiped the foam from around my mouth with her sleeve.

I never took one of anything in my life. I suppose that's obvious by now. I didn't want to get fat, so what I'd taken to doing was drinking incredible quantities of water and other nonalcoholic liquids. I was Mr. Hydrated, king of the urinals.

So there I was in the bathroom when Perry showed up next to me.

"That was quite a speech in there." Verna had met him a few times, but I'd only met Perry once before, when we went to Kathy's place for takeout Middle Eastern food.

"So, you come here a lot?"

"Whenever I have to go."

I zipped up and went over to wash my hands. "Touché. I meant the meeting house."

He quickly turned serious. "Yes, yes, I do. It's the one place left in the world where it's okay to be slow. You're encouraged to take your time. Don't you think we need that? I screwed up a lot by not taking my time."

He sounded like Verna talking to me in bed. I was wiping my hands on the rough brown paper towels. "You're right about that, bro." I said. I thought of some other stuff to say to him. Like about stoner boy. But Mitch pushed open the door, and I knew it was time to take my leave. If I didn't get out soon, stoner boy would be walking in too, and then something would be hitting the fan.

■ ■ ■

It had been like rehab—less meanness, but less honesty, too. Nobody else really said what they felt besides the son and Kathy's father, but I guess that seems pretty good for an average day. Chalk one up for the Friends meeting house, after all. Me, I could never say what I really felt. That's why I always started in on the other shit. I know that's a lame excuse. At rehab, when anyone said something like that, some people would start snickering. Or a big "Awwww" would go up from one of the returnees.

When I got back to the reception area, it had cleared out quickly. Kathy was standing with Verna, who was holding a couple of clumpy napkins in her hand that I assumed held pieces of wedding cake. Verna took comfort in traditions like that—traditions she knew had no meaning or impact. She was planning a trip for us back to the City of Murals, a romantic weekend in Stupidville. Talk about an oxymoron. But I loved that about her—her faith in the ridiculous.

"Kathy, sorry about opening up my mouth," I said, suddenly feeling shy and stupid, like I was apologizing again for something I did while I was drunk or stoned. Not in my right mind. But I *was* in my right mind. As right as it got these days.

"That's okay. It'll give everyone something to talk about. I appreciate it, Silver. It came from that weird little heart of yours."

Verna squeezed my arm. We made a quick move to the door. Somebody else grabbed my arm.

"What about the mural?" he asked. He looked like Dean Martin.

"Check it out," I said. "I think you'll like it."

With our sick muffler coughing noisily, we pulled out onto the street. I saw a heavyset redhead in a muumuu-type dress sitting in the driver's seat of a dirty red sedan. She was parked on the street, facing the Society of Friends.

"See that?" I said to Verna as we passed the car.

"What? Her?"

"I think that's her."

"You think that's her?"

I slammed into reverse and backed up the car. It wasn't safe for anyone to be sitting for long in a car on that street, even an ex-wife with who-knows-what on her mind. For it must have been her—she was sobbing. She looked positively pitiful and wretched. And Verna and I had both been equally wretched in our lives, so we knew what wretched looked like.

"Don't just stare at her," Verna said.

I rolled down the window. "Don't shoot them," I said.

She waved her hand at us. I think she might've even smiled.

"Does that mean she *is* gonna shoot them, or she isn't?" I asked Verna.

"She's not gonna shoot anybody," Verna said. "Now, let's get out of here.

I was never good at retracing my steps, and all the bombed-out streets looked kind of the same to me, so we quickly got lost, then slowly found our way home.

"Verna, why didn't you say anything at the wedding?" I asked as we pulled in front of our tiny shotgun house on the flats near the old warehouses.

"Silver," she said to me, "you had to learn to speak up, and I had to learn to shut up."

I wasn't quite sure what she meant, but it seemed like the kind of statement that did not want any follow-up.

The driver's-side door had to be kicked violently in order to shut it, so I gave it my usual boot, but in my new dress shoes, purchased specially for the occasion, I slipped and fell to the street.

"Are you okay, big boy?" Verna said, bending down to lift me up. I was reminded again of how strong she was. How strong she had been for me. I took her in my arms, and we began to sway back and forth into a slow dance right there on our sad little street. It'd been a long time since we didn't need any music for that.

"Do Mormons dance?" I asked.

"It's Quakers, asshole," she said.

Closing Costs

Eric sat at the ornate dining-room table they'd inherited from the house's previous owner. It came with six chairs, one with big arms on the sides. "For the man of the house," Sammy had told him with a wink. Sammy's wife, Josephine, had died the year before, and alone in that big house, he no longer needed the big chair to establish his position. Eric wondered if old Sammy missed that uncomfortable chair, if he sometimes lowered his heavy arms in anticipation, only to have them fall dangling to his sides, just another body in another chair at Sterling Gardens, the retirement home where he now lived.

The problem with the chair was that the arms bumped the table so you couldn't pull it in close. You ended up either bending over and lunging at your food or watching it fall off your fork on the long journey. If that's what being the man of the house meant, Eric didn't want any part of it.

What were they thinking, buying a house? There was no one to ask just now, two A.M., sitting across from the big chair that he refused to sit in. The stress of the move had caused an increase in the dosage of one of Ellen's pills. She was upstairs sleeping her drugged sleep like a large, immovable rock, leaving him to ponder the mistake of the big stupid house they could never imagine filling together.

With no one around to frown or grimace, Eric slurped his cereal noisily. The last time he'd gone home to visit his family in Detroit, he'd had breakfast with his ninety-three-year-old grandfather, who was staying at his parents' after nearly burning his own house down. They were in a holding pattern—what to do with Grandpa? He sat at the kitchen table, half-deaf, eating his cereal with a variety of slurps and snorts that finally forced Eric from the room.

"I say put him in a home. How can you stand it?" he'd said to his father.

"You can't institutionalize someone for bad table manners," his father said.

His mother was reduced to a permanent teeth-gritting grimace. It wasn't *her* father—he'd had the wisdom to die before he became so much trouble. Eric cut his visit short. He had to get back for the closing on the house in Flint. His mother was anxious to visit once they settled in. "And next you're getting married, right?" she shouted as he drove away.

Ellen rarely visited his parents with him. They wouldn't let them sleep together "under their roof," though he and Ellen had been living together for five years. She'd stay with her sister and join them for an awkward dinner before they headed back to Flint. Eric vowed to look up the laws on common-law marriages—maybe he could convince his folks to let up a bit. After all, he and Ellen were home owners now, and that should count for something.

"Sammy, Sammy," Eric sighed as he scooped out the last few Golden Nuggets from the bottom of the bowl, "I'm slurping cereal like an old man." Sammy and his wife had had no children—no one to fret over him now. He was enormously obese, and Eric guessed that the distance from the chair to the table would have been perfect for him. "Sammy, I can't even fill up your chair." He liked hearing his own voice in the big, spooky house. He had taped a pair of sunglasses on a ceramic vase of a woman's head that Sammy had left behind. He called it Marge. It sat on the window ledge in the kitchen. They were hanging on to all of Sammy's junk to keep the place from seeming like their own.

Eric and Ellen were both in their mid-thirties and beyond the years in which marriage was even discussed—they simply weren't in love enough anymore. Everything was already cemented into dull routine, and if the routine had cracks, they had learned to step over them. Ellen had been married once, right out of high school. She'd moved to Toledo with her husband, and he had abused her till she fled back to suburban Detroit. The idea of any kind of wedding made them both shudder. It bound them stubbornly together. That, and their decision not to have children.

Eric had come out of college thinking he was unconventional—the romantic outsider, the rebellious joker, the life of any party. One thing about being unconventional, it doesn't put bread on the table. After college, no one indulged him anymore. All his druggie friends were cutting their hair, putting putty in their nose-ring holes, covering their tattoos with long sleeves, getting jobs. After seven years of off-and-on study, a double major in philosophy and English got Eric a job selling cars. He stopped calling himself a Marxist.

He'd met Ellen at a large party thrown by his cousin Ned, a mid-level drug dealer. When the police arrived to break things up, Eric and Ellen, stoned and drunk, left together and spent the night at his apartment. Soon they were living together and throwing lively parties of their own. He loved to watch her argue. She'd take on anybody on anything, and she was smart—smart like someone who'd escaped a death sentence. She acted like she knew more than the rest of them, and Eric believed she did.

They'd left that apartment long ago. They didn't dance anymore. Loud music hurt Eric's ears. Ellen wanted to stay home, but
she didn't know what she wanted to *do* there. Many of their friends
were becoming parents, and Eric knew what *they* were doing at
home—changing diapers, getting spit up on, staying up all night with
sick kids. Who needed that? But Ellen needed a new something.
He needed a new something. To collect. To pursue. For a while,
it had been the house, days spent wandering the city in the real
estate agent's car while she prattled on about the features of this
or that house.

The big chair asserted its presence across from him. Eric could
imagine his arms strapped to it, getting electrocuted. *Slurp, slurp.*
His last meal. He lifted the bowl and drank the rest of the milk. It
dribbled down his chin. He wiped it with the sleeve of his robe, then
rose and went back to bed. "Good night, Marge," he said, patting
her head as he passed through the kitchen.

"I had the flying dream again last night," Ellen said as they lay
together in bed the next morning. For weeks, she'd been dreaming
she could fly. Eric had never, ever once dreamed he was flying.
Not that he could remember, anyway. He half-sneered. "Where'd
you go this time?"

"Nowhere. Just from room to room, up and down the stairs."

"See, we've got it all here—you don't need to fly anywhere."

"It wasn't this house."

"Oh," he said. He knew she wanted him to ask more, but he
wasn't biting. "I dreamed I was building a deck," he said, though
it wasn't true. Building a deck was something they talked about to
make conversation. It was like watching a half-amusing sitcom—it
got them through the silence of the house some nights. The truth
was, he'd dreamed he was moving again, struggling unsuccessfully
to fit a lot of little boxes into one big box. An old girlfriend, not
Ellen, was helping him.

"Eric, it's cold in here. Maybe the furnace is out." Ellen wrapped the comforter tightly around her. Winter had come early to Flint—not even November, and it'd already snowed a half-dozen times.

The furnace had been a sticking point. It was old and needed replacing. Sammy wouldn't budge. He threw in the table and chairs, which he didn't need in his furnished condo, anyway, but the furnace was nonnegotiable. Eric and Ellen didn't have enough money for a furnace after the down payment, after all the closing costs and moving expenses. What was Sammy going to do with all that money—their money—in Sterling Gardens?

Eric got out of bed and held his hand to the radiator beneath the window: hot. Relieved, he sat down on it and warmed his skinny butt. "Furnace is on," he said firmly.

"Listen, all I know is it's cold in here," she said.

"It's an old house. It's drafty," he said. He wanted to stop being mean to her, to try to understand why life both wasn't enough and was too much for her. He wanted to have a good argument with her just to see her animated again, confident and not afraid. It seemed like they could barely talk in that house, much less be intimate. He wanted to bring in an exorcist to clear the air. He was cold, even sitting on the radiator, so he went downstairs to check the thermostat. At the bottom of the stairs, he felt a chill of panic at the broken window on the landing.

■ ■ ■

Though they'd been in the house for six months, they'd left most of their belongings in boxes in the living room. Upstairs, they'd unpacked clothes and filled closets, but they were slow to unpack all the *stuff*—the books, knickknacks, Ellen's stack of paintings from when she used to paint, Eric's beer can collection from his college days.

He stepped into the disorder of their living room and didn't know where to begin. How would they ever figure out what was missing? Beer cans were strewn everywhere. He couldn't believe he hadn't heard anything after he'd gone back to bed. Maybe he had—he wasn't used to the house's noises and wouldn't know what to be alarmed by. Nothing could have roused Ellen.

"Ellen," he said evenly, "come on down. We've been robbed."

She rushed down in her old ratty robe, then saw the broken window and ran back upstairs. He sat in the dining room in the big chair, his hands firmly gripping the armrests, the jolts rushing through him.

"They're gone. It's safe to come down."

"Don't touch anything!" she shouted down the stairs. "Call the police. I'm getting dressed."

"Shouldn't we figure out what's missing first?" he asked. "What's the protocol here? I mean, won't that be the first thing the cops ask?"

"Call the cops," she said. "I'm getting dressed."

Eric called 911 and began to take stock. Their laptops. The TV, VCR, DVD, CD player and CDs—everything with initials, that would be easy enough to remember. They didn't have much else of value. Eric had a lot of books from when he used to read philosophy and poetry. Those heavy boxes sat untouched in a corner. He wished they'd hauled them away—he knew he'd never look at them again.

When he looked around, all he saw were remnants of who they used to be. Things that meant something once. Sentimental attachments. A box of all the gag gifts they'd given each other. Eric remembered the plastic banana that turned into a dildo that he'd given Ellen back when they both had a sense of humor—he hoped the cops weren't going to go through *everything.* A jack-in-the-box from the old toy box his grandfather used to keep for him when he came to visit. His old gold-plated cocaine kit, a birthday gift from

Ellen, was probably somewhere in the chaos. If he could find it himself, maybe he could scrape together enough residue for one snort. His mind was cluttering with all the *junk*—he wished they'd taken everything. Ellen came down the stairs, still shivering. Eric stood and grabbed a tablecloth from the floor and covered the broken window with it.

"Should we clean up the glass?" he asked.

"Wait for the police," she said. "You did call them?"

"Yeah, I called."

"What's missing?" she asked. She was dressed in work clothes—a navy skirt and white blouse—as if she wanted to insist it was going to be an ordinary day. But then she suddenly pulled him to her and hugged him tightly. Eric didn't know what was in that hug, but he squeezed back just as tightly. All he felt was a stifling numbness.

"All the electronic stuff." Eric leaned back and rubbed his hands over Sammy's fuzzy red wallpaper. Ellen continued clutching his waist.

"What else did we have?" she asked. "What's in all these boxes, anyway?"

"They took everything," he said, just to say it, to be melodramatic. Lately, he'd felt like there wasn't enough drama of any kind in their lives, and when something did happen, it was like he was seeing it through a filter, as if he, too, were on drugs that numbed the senses. Moving had given him a backache, but even that went away quickly. What was their excuse? Could they write each other notes for emotional absence? "What's with the wallpaper?" she asked. He immediately brought his hands back to his sides. He shrugged. "It's fuzzy," he said.

"You're fuzzy," she said. "I see they left your beer cans." She almost sneered. He pulled away from her and picked one off the floor to crush it in his hands, but it was one of the older, thicker cans, and all he could do was bend it in half. Was he really someone who had a beer can collection? Would he be remembered for that?

"Yeah, I know. It's pitiful," he said. "What was I thinking?" he asked aloud.

"What were we thinking?" she asked.

"When?"

"When we moved all this junk. Let's just take it to the curb."

Moving from an apartment to a big house, they hadn't felt they needed to go through and weed things out—they'd just tossed everything in boxes and brought it here. Some boxes had been dumped, some untouched, and others just opened and left.

Ellen went into the kitchen to make coffee. Eric went upstairs to dress. If the police came soon, maybe they could both get in half a day of work. He put on his blue suit and the red tie his brother had given him for Christmas. A power tie, his brother the engineer had called it, appreciating Eric's new conformity, rubbing it in a little.

Ellen taught at the neighborhood preschool. Their friends thought that was funny, since they had no interest in having kids, but Ellen said she felt safe there. Eric had always wanted to go to work with her, to watch her with kids, but she refused to let him.

They would both have to call in soon. Let their bosses know what was up. Eric's hair was thinning, though he could still comb over what would soon be a bald spot. He was too young to be having a midlife crisis, unless he was going to die pretty early. He wondered if it was a relationship crisis, or simultaneous personal crises.

"Didn't you hear anything? Remember when we used to take drugs because we wanted to, not because we had to?" he shouted, angry at their sad boxes of junk rejected by thieves. Ellen had saved all her old high school and college papers, all with A's on them, in an old Xerox-paper box he rested his feet on.

Eric didn't even smoke pot anymore. He thought it took the edge off, the edge he needed to be aggressive and sell lots of cars.

He was good at it. He had a great spiel about how a new car could change your life. He had theories of fitting cars to personalities. The other salesmen called him Doctor Eric. He specialized in selling cars to nutcases. Business was booming. He thought Ellen needed a new car, though they couldn't afford it.

He had been sure the house would work as a symbol of starting over again, together—something solid. He imagined them stripping wallpaper, painting, decorating, a deck, a garden. He never dreamed they'd be unable to even unpack.

His father said the fire had given him an excuse to get rid of his grandfather's accumulated junk. "Junk, pure junk," his father marveled. Was Eric a collector like his grandfather? Why couldn't he just sit in the room and listen to the old man eat? Eric half-wished his grandfather would die—his house stank like an old dog. He was surprised by his own cruelty. Where would it lead him? He imagined Sammy and his grandfather sitting together, talking about his lack of gratitude. His insolence.

He decided Ellen was right. He'd throw everything away, carry the remaining boxes to the curb unexamined. "Too much junk!" he shouted aloud. He had to retie his tie three times before the length was right. He decided to throw out the big chair with the arms, too. Somebody else's idea of being a man. All the other chairs were armless, waiting for definition.

"Goddamn it!" she shouted back, "They even had a fucking snack before they left. Didn't they know we were right upstairs? How can we stay here now? Burglars coming in and having a god-damn snack. Nobody told me about this. I thought it was a safe neighborhood."

Eric shivered at the thought of someone watching them sleep—a true violation. What did they look like together? He'd noticed with alarm that he could not fall asleep unless he lay on his side turned away from her. He thought it had something to do with which side his heart was on. Maybe his heart didn't like all that weight on it. He remembered the sweet drool at the corner of her mouth that first night they slept together. He'd woken her with breakfast in bed. He was embarrassed at how warm and vulnerable he used to be. He liked being on the edge now. Sharp. Aggressive. Taking on all comers. A fucking home owner. He was going to pay off the mortgage early, buy a second home. Maybe a boat. He always wanted a boat. New big things, not all that trash. He thought of his own car in the driveway—he assumed it was still there—a Honda Civic, sky blue. He used to pride himself on fixing his own cars. Now he just got a new one every few years.

"What did they have?" he asked. He was hungry with shock. He wanted to eat enough to feel permanent.

"A Coke and some chips," she said. "And there's a raw egg in the frying pan."

"Maybe we spooked them." He looked down at the egg, its yellow eye staring back up at him. "Will our insurance cover that?" He laughed too loudly at his own joke. They'd like this story at work. He could use it. He looked over at the Marge figurine and winked at her. Sammy was safe somewhere, probably still asleep. Eric imagined him cranking the thermostat up in Sterling Gardens, thinking of the money he'd saved by not giving in and getting a new furnace for the house. He was going to take a sledgehammer to that chair, his first home improvement project.

"Oh, yeah," Ellen said. "Call the insurance company. Right away."

Instead, he turned on the burner and started to cook the egg.

"What are you doing?" she said. "That's evidence." He thought she was making a joke, but she stared at him, haunted and pale in her bright work clothes.

Eric went on cooking. One pure, simple thing. The police would be arriving soon, or maybe they'd take hours. He didn't know the priority given to a break-in in their neighborhood. He used to think that if he loved her more, loved her better, she wouldn't need her medication. Now he didn't know if he had the capacity to change her in any positive way. He heard a siren in the distance, but it abruptly stopped.

Owning the house was almost the same as being married. It would make splitting up messy and complicated. Neither of them had the energy for that, either. Or the desire, he thought. Hoped. Wondered. He didn't want to be an old man alone. He was the man of the house, and he was going to hold on to—on to what? What would they replace the junk with? The egg was sizzling.

"Hey, we're alive," he said. "Do you want one?"

She shook her head. She was watching the coffee drift down into the carafe. They were lost to each other in their own simple things. "Sunny side up," he said to himself, "or over easy?"

Marathon Dance

A thin, bare branch in the tree out back was bent down like a catapult, weighed down by a large, unruly nest. What bird would build such a large nest? On bad days, Ava imagined climbing up there, curling up and waiting for the warmth and shelter of the underside of a wing.

She knew few birds by sight—robin, cardinal, blue jay, ones everybody knew. This was the nest of a big fucking bird, she thought. Or perhaps the nest had been abandoned years ago. She didn't even know what kind of *tree* it was.

For a long time, they'd been unsure about keeping it—the baby. They could no longer be unsure. It was March, though it still felt like February, that endless gray Midwest February she remembered from her childhood. She stared out the sliding glass door. The tree blotted her view of the neighbors' empty deck that faced theirs. The neighbor whose name she did not know. Every condo in their development was burdened with an identical redwood deck, as if they were a fleet of boats sailing in unison toward the same destination. Except the wind had died. Except they had no sails. Or motors. Or oars.

Three months ago, they'd moved to Rochester Hills in suburban Detroit—her, Robin, and Baby X—from Florida, where they'd lived on one of the Bay Harbor Islands north of Miami. She had hoped they'd be stranded there forever in paradise, the tollbooth scanner silently registering each trip on the bridge back and forth from the mainland. Every so often, she or Robin had to stop by the bridge office to buy more trips for the bar code on their windshield. Ava reckoned they had about thirty more trips left if they ever got back down there.

■ ■ ■

"Hey," Robin said, bending down to peck her on the forehead like some condescending politician kissing his mother for the cameras. More and more, Robin acted as though a camera were on him—careful, sticking to a script he'd written out for himself and wasn't sharing with her.

"Greetings, Future Father of America," Ava said, continuing to stare out the large, clear glass.

"Ouch," he said, taking a crisp step back.

You don't know the meaning of ouch, she wanted to say. "Did you ever notice the big nest in that tree out back?" she asked.

"What?" He glanced up quickly, then back at her. "No. I gotta run—what's for dinner?"

"The truth hurts," she said, not able, finally, to let him go without comment, though he was halfway to the bedroom, so she had to shout. She heard his thick belt buckle clunk against the carpet as he changed into his running clothes.

"You can run, but you can't hide!" she shouted. She had to work harder and harder to get any reaction from him. He was in another time zone, an alternative reality where she wasn't six months pregnant.

He came out in his little silky magenta jogging shorts and tight

T-shirt. She'd bought him a pair of black tights to keep his legs warm, but he never wore them.

"Have you been drinking?" he asked, tilting his head accusingly.

"There's a thought," she replied. "I hear it's good for fetal tissue."

"This sucks," he said, and while she floated on a thin smile, he disappeared out the front door. She got up and stood at the living-room window to watch him stretch, pushing against the young tree out front as if he could topple it. She fogged the window with her breath and drew a tiny smiley face with the long, painted nail of her middle finger.

She wanted a wet, sloppy kiss from someone, and it didn't have to be Robin. In Miami, he wouldn't get a second look in those shorts, but in Michigan, in March, he looked ridiculous.

■ ■ ■

Robin had been transferred to Detroit by Aata-Ride, a Southern car rental company that was going national. In between getting news of his transfer and discovering she was pregnant, Ava had considered cutting ties and staying behind in Miami. She'd gotten her degree in hotel and restaurant management from Florida International and was a manager at the Blue Moon, a trendy, funky hotel on Miami Beach. It was a simple life there, handling the credit cards of the beautiful people.

Of course, his first response was "You're *what?*" But once the fact was established, there was no sitcom remedy or soap opera drama. They'd been living together in Miami for four years, though it had always seemed like a tenuous arrangement—no pledges of fidelity, no marriage plans. Ava herself had something on the side for nearly half their time together—a businessman who stayed at the Blue Moon when he was in town. Convenient for them both.

Then he either stopped traveling or found another hotel, she wasn't sure which.

Their friends called them the Pragmatics—there'd never been a romance in any traditional sense. They'd fallen in together casually and had been content to keep their money separate and their hearts subtly coated. She'd lost her health insurance when they moved, so they had to have a quickie marriage with strangers as witnesses to get her on his policy.

"Shit, what are you going to do?" he'd said. In a panic, she had called him at work from the hallway outside the doctor's office. She immediately realized that was a mistake. She needed to see his face. Next to the phone was an evacuation plan for the building in case of emergency. She traced her route from the red dot.

"Ava?"

"What are *we* going to do, right? It's not just me. I think I want to have it. Let's keep it."

"Ava. Ava, can we talk about this later?"

"We sure can," she said, and hung up. She began to lean her forehead toward the wall but then saw a dark smudge right where her head would hit. She wondered how many others had leaned their heads against this wall in wonder or despair. She fished for her keys and held them tight in her fist as she headed out to the parking lot. It took her ten minutes to find her car.

■ ■ ■

They lived in apartment number 9, on the second floor in the far corner of the building. At night they could sit on the cement walkway and look out over the canal at the backyards of the expensive homes on the other island. The old woman who'd lived in number 9 before them had fallen off the balcony to her death.

Ava waited for him in her cheap plastic porch chair, ignoring the lush pink sunset. The air-conditioning unit hummed and whooshed directly below her. It was muggy for November, which was usually the start of the Months of Heaven—from November to March, when it was 80 degrees and clear every day.

In an earlier life, she'd been an exotic dancer at an upscale "gentleman's retreat," Club Elite, on Biscayne Boulevard. When her mother came from Wisconsin to visit, Ava told her she was waitressing. In the years since, she'd never run into any of the regulars from the Elite. She liked that about Miami—you could re-create yourself quickly and without baggage. She'd moved there to start over and was able to start over yet again, without even moving.

She heard the creak of the iron gate at the bottom of the stairs, then Robin's key in their mailbox. He knew she always picked up the mail, yet he checked it daily. In case she forgot, in case she missed something. It was that way with him—always hoping for some unlikely good news.

He trudged up the steps. She stood up. She didn't want to appear to be pouncing on him, but she couldn't wait. She wanted to try to put words to the jumbled ache inside that was strangling her with desire to have a child. To start over one more time. He turned the corner. She rushed over and hugged him.

"A fucking baby," he said. He laughed, and she did not like the sound of that laugh—like a choking dog's gasp.

"I'm thirty-seven," she said, pulling back from him.

"I heard about this kind of thing. It's all about math."

"It's not about math," she said firmly. She kicked him in the shins, suddenly and viciously.

"Ouch. What the hell?"

"Must be premenopausal reflexes."

"I'm not ready."

"Robin, you're never going to be ready."

"That's the truth."

"I don't want to have another abortion."

He paused. "How many have you had?"

"A couple."

"Hey, how'd this happen?" he asked suddenly. Condoms were their method of contraception.

"I don't know, you tell me. You're the father, in case you're wondering."

"Oh, that's a relief," he said sarcastically. "When does bad luck become stupidity?"

"When you're the father."

■ ■ ■

The spare room in the condo would not be spare for long—it would be Baby X's room. Ava never liked her own name, though Robin had pointed out that if she were a company, her name would be near the front of the phone book. Her last name was Zelinski. His was Roberts. Ava imagined her parents had gotten one of those books of names and gotten bored before they even got through the A's. She knew they'd have to stop calling the baby It. They knew it was going to be a boy, so they could name it now, but she thought that'd be bad luck, and Robin was in no hurry to make anything more real than it already was.

Robin meted out blame as part of his exercise regimen. And she was to blame for the pregnancy, and for refusing to end it. He said she was blackmailing him into becoming a father, that it was a dirty trick to pull, right when his career was on the move. He couldn't, wouldn't, put her out on the street, but he could certainly make her life miserable. Ava was hoping the fact of the baby's birth might soften him up, though looking beyond the birth was like staring into the Miami sun—she had to shield her eyes and turn away.

■ ■ ■

Robin was smooth in a way that did not cut it in Detroit. He was having trouble getting off the ground with his new coworkers. Some of them took to calling him "Bobbin' Robin," the name of a local DJ of some repute who'd been arrested for having sex with a female impersonator in a car at the foot of the Ambassador Bridge. She had not met any of his coworkers. He had not cared that she used to be a stripper, but now he was embarrassed by her pregnancy. She felt incredibly isolated in the odd symmetric sprawl of their condo complex. There were no sidewalks, so she had to walk in the street to go anywhere. Everybody drove everywhere in Detroit. She imagined the smirks Robin got in his little neon jogging shorts.

Ava had grown up in Milwaukee with guys like the guys Robin had working for him—he didn't understand their odd mix of stubborn pride and stubborn laziness. He ranted and raved about them on a regular basis when he came home at night. Robin was taxiing down the runway, looking for a way up, a way out. He'd finally opted for ground transportation—he was training for the Detroit Marathon in May, running every day after work.

■ ■ ■

Ava turned on the oven to heat up the mac and cheese casserole she'd made that morning from her mother's recipe. Comfort food, her mother called it. As the streetlights began to glow softly, Robin came striding in the door, all blustery, exaggerating his fitness.

"Have a good run?" she asked. She'd nearly forgotten about being mad at him.

"Oh, yeah," he said, looking at his runner's wristwatch. He poked at its tiny buttons, and it made a series of beeps. He nodded to himself.

"That might come in handy to time the contractions," she said, placing the casserole on their glass-topped kitchen table. The oven mitts were in the shape of Michigan's Lower Peninsula, a parting gift from Molly, a friend from Miami who worked as a flight attendant for Northwest.

"I was thinking of naming the baby Spatula," she said as she lifted a chunk of the casserole onto his plate.

"Spatula's a girl's name," he said without missing a beat.

"Maybe it'll be twins. A boy and a girl, Corkscrew and Spatula. We could call him Corkie and her Pat."

"Spat," he said. She noticed that he really didn't seem out of breath or sweaty.

■ ■ ■

When she'd met him on a singles cruise to the Bahamas, he'd insisted she call him Robin, not Rob.

"What's wrong with Rob?" she asked above the sound system blaring old disco tunes that used to accompany her while she stripped.

"Rob? Rob as in steal? Everyone I should never have trusted called me Rob."

She liked his abrasive edge. She, too, had come to distrust the false, easy intimacies of her earlier life. Everything came with a price. Men sticking dollar bills into her G-string with their teeth, they wanted their money's worth, and that got defined a lot of different ways.

Ava slept in his tiny cabin the first night, and every night of the cruise. Dark wavy hair. Clear skin. Muscular. Unattached, not interested in attachment. Funny. Confident. Five years younger. Smooth. Robin, not Rob. He wouldn't steal anything from her.

When she wanted to piss him off, she called him Rob. Or Robby. There was no nickname or shortening of Ava. Ava was Ava, frontward and backward.

■ ■ ■

She sat watching Robin wolfing down his mac and cheese. "Carbo-loading," he called it for the umpteenth time, his mouth full of orange noodles. She had no appetite herself. The cliché of "eating for two" did not seem to apply. She found herself forcing food down for the baby's sake. He had four books on running marathons. She had one on pregnancy, *What to Expect When You're Expecting*. It went month by month. His marathon books went week by week. Both in preparation for the Big Day.

After dinner, he headed straight to the bathroom for a long shower. She dozed off on the couch, and when she awoke, it was morning. The afghan Teri had made for her had been carelessly thrown over her. Teri, her sister, was dying of breast cancer at age thirty-two. A lesbian in White River, Wisconsin, she had faced her share of adversity. But dying, that was a whole different thing.

Ava's toes were cold. Robin was in the shower again. Or still, for all she knew. She stuck her head into the bathroom. "Save some hot water for me!" she shouted through the steam. She saw his bathing cap poke out from behind the curtain. He was slowly going bald and thought the cap would keep his hair from falling out.

■ ■ ■

It was late, or early, in those indistinct hours between two and six A.M. Ava lay in bed with a sour stomach. Robin had stayed up watching a basketball game from the West Coast. He could stay up forever and still seem alert the next day. Despite his thinning hair, he bristled with youth and intensity. Robin had slipped into bed and curled away from her on the far edge of their king-size water bed, where he now slept his usual seamless sleep. She sniffed the air, then sniffed again, panicked, as if she smelled smoke. Since Ava'd become pregnant, all her senses had intensified. She became

nauseated merely smelling french fries. What she smelled now was
the scent of another woman. Messy sex smells. She froze. Her heart
thudded heavily in her chest, and in her head. Robin had opted out
of his usual shower after his run to work on his laptop.

Ava braced herself, then slowly slipped out of bed. It rocked a
bit, but Robin simply floated on the waves. She moved to his side,
bent her face to his boxers, and took a deep whiff. No question
about it. She rushed to the bathroom and bent over the toilet, but
she did not throw up. If she really loved him, she would've thrown
up, she thought.

■ ■ ■

"How'd you find somebody else to fuck so soon?" she asked. "I
mean, you can't even get your workers to go out for a beer after
work, but you've found somebody else to fuck!" She shouted the
last four words, as if another voice had emerged, overtaken the dull
cynic. Something raw, unfiltered, organic, but bad for the baby.

"How am I supposed to answer a question like that?"

"Truthfully." She didn't remember March being this cold
in Wisconsin. Tulips should be blooming. Or at least crocuses.
Something erupting into bloom out of the hard ground. She was
staring out through the glass at the tree with the big empty nest.

"Damn it, I'm lonely. You've been blaming all this shit on me
and acting like an old married person. I know, officially we *are*
married, but neither of us wanted this—this soap opera in suburban
fucking Detroit."

"They've never set a soap opera in Detroit. No glamour."

"It'd be too violent," he said. He was willing to seriously discuss
the idea of a soap opera in Detroit but not the child on its way,
third trimester.

"You're just horny, don't get the two things confused. Try mas-
turbation," she said.

"Adoption," he said. "I miss the ocean."

"Why don't you just hire a prostitute for a few months?" She didn't mean this. The conversation was getting away from her. She couldn't muster the indignation of the betrayed, though she knew she had the world's implicit sympathy. "'MAN CHEATS ON PREGNANT WIFE—details at 11.' I can't stay up that late. Tell me now so I know what I'm up against."

"You're not up against anything."

"Why don't we have any baby furniture? Huh? Why don't you read something about what I'm going through instead of . . . I can't believe you were out fucking when I thought you were running. No wonder you never get cold in those little shorts. Easy on, easy off. The long showers—it's all making sense now."

"Wait a minute," Robin said. "You're not being fair. I started out running."

"And?"

"And I found someone to run with . . ."

"Ha!"

"And . . . wait! And we stopped at her house one day afterward . . ."

"Is she married?"

"Irrelevant."

"Not irrelevant! Me and the baby need a home. At least until I can get it together and find a job to take care of us." Ava had frequently gone over her options, smearing the glass-topped table with moist fingerprints.

Her college degree would be nearly worthless in Detroit, which was not exactly a tourist mecca. Worst-case scenario, she could return to dancing. Pushing forty but not over the hill. Though she swore she'd never be stripping with stretch marks in one of those seedy places. She'd only danced in big, well-lit places with polite, enormous bouncers dressed in suits.

She could take the baby and go back to Miami or back to Wisconsin. Wisconsin meant defeat. Miami meant high risk—just the two of them, with no assurance Robin would send support checks.

"You've got a home here as long as you want one," he said. "But what if I start liking the kid?" he asked suddenly, as if she wasn't there.

"He's your kid. You're going to love him, trust me. I'll move out as soon as I can, but I don't know when that'll be, or to where. . . . Molly's going to fly up to be my Lamaze coach."

"Wait—I could do that," he said.

"Yes, you could," she said. "You could also show up at the hospital with your new girlfriend."

"I wouldn't do that," he said flatly. "I know everybody says this, but it's nothing serious. I was going to tell you."

"Run your fucking marathon," she said, and stormed into the empty baby's room, where she lay on the thick carpet and fell asleep while practicing her breathing exercises.

■　■　■

On Sunday, Robin made her breakfast in bed, spilling orange juice over the newspaper and her ratty white nightgown. They were exhausted from arguing and could barely finish their sentences. She was dying for a cup of coffee, but she wasn't supposed to have caffeine. After she showered, he took her to Babyland down in the city. It turned out to be located at a notorious drug-dealing intersection. But it had the biggest ad in the Yellow Pages, and that meant something to Robin. They brushed past a tall, nodding man leaning against a newspaper box. Ava nodded back. Everyone was her ally today. They loaded up Robin's Trans Am with so much gear that they had to tie the trunk closed.

"I'm not as big of a jerk as you want me to be," he said, back at the condo, unloading a stash that included a crib, a bassinet, a swing, and a new device called a Diaper Genie that twisted soiled diapers into giant sanitary rosary beads.

She thought about that for a minute. Did she *want* him to be a jerk? She'd shut him out since she'd told him she wanted to keep the baby and he'd tried to talk her out of it. She'd left him stranded in his tiny magenta shorts in a world of large automobiles and resentful coworkers.

"I don't want you to be a jerk," she said softly, resting a hand on his shoulder while he jiggled the swing out of the tightly packed trunk.

"Motorized," he said. "Not like all those old crank ones."

"Everything's got to be motorized here."

"That's why they brought me in—'Aata Ride to the Rescue!'"

"We've got to start talking positive about this baby," Ava said, collapsing on the couch as Robin carried in a stack of large boxes and dropped them on the floor.

"I just . . . I just don't *want* a kid."

"*I* just want a kid. You know in your heart of hearts you want to be a father, so why the big denial thing?"

He started tearing open the boxes, but he quickly realized he needed tools. He had no tools. He collapsed back onto the couch next to her, staring upward, his head tilted back over the rear cushions. "It's us. Things are so shaky."

"But we've been together for years. Things have always been shaky."

"A baby isn't shaky, though. Shaky doesn't work with babies." Robin's parents had gotten divorced when he was twelve—right when he was mad at them for everything anyway, they gave him a reason to stay mad forever.

"Why do you think we've stuck it out this long?" Ava asked. They'd stayed together through years of warily protecting their own spaces, through long stretches of quiet tension broken by the occasional night of wild sex and easy laughter. Why? They were like low-powered magnets—just enough attraction to hold each other in their fields but not enough to link them.

"Maybe we should start doing drugs again," Robin said. "We were pretty happy when we were stoned."

"Refresh my memory. Christ, Robby, I'm pregnant! Pregnant! Look around you—bassinet, changing table, crib. Fucking Diaper Genie!"

"I think I'm going to like Diaper Genie," he said. "Will it grant us wishes?" She punched him hard in the shoulder, but he only laughed.

■ ■ ■

"Well, it's your fault for going for the young stud," Teri told her. She was on her deathbed and not mincing words. Teri's life had always seemed distant to Ava, an abstract concept she could never grasp. Teri had been a successful lawyer, ambition her pure buzz.

Teri had been living in Marquette, near the icy waters of Lake Superior, but had returned to Milwaukee to die, and Ava was there to say good-bye. At the end, Teri had no one to care for her. She wasn't going to die in a hospital, so she'd gone home. Their mother had taken over, invigorated by being needed again.

"After dancing for those fat old horny jerks all those years . . ." Ava began, but drifted off.

"Surprised you didn't end up like me," Teri said. "It's not too late, you know."

"Yeah, I'll be a single lesbian mom—that sounds real attractive."

"Hey, I know a few," Teri protested. "Listen, Ava, you want me to go there and kick the little punk's ass?"

Ava laughed. "You'll have to catch him first. He's running at least as far as her house, wherever she lives."

"Mom could catch him." Teri laughed.

"Mom thinks he *is* a catch," Ava said. Their mother had no idea of the complex nature of Ava's marriage to Robin and was simply ecstatic over becoming a grandmother. "What am I supposed to do, jog behind him, six months pregnant, without him seeing me? That's the beauty of his scheme."

"He's not smart enough to scheme."

"Oh, he's smart. He just skims the surface of things. He thinks he can walk on water. In Miami, we could hide in all the palm trees and bright colors. We had our separate lives between the beach and the mainland. Nothing seemed permanent, even marriage. It's just one big filled-in swamp, after all. In Detroit, everything's so permanent it's turning to rust. Robin doesn't do rust."

"Why are you having this baby? I mean, *this* baby, his baby?"

"Good genes?" Ava said dubiously. She didn't want to explain it to Teri, to Robin, to anyone—to put the words of her desire out there where they might fall apart under scrutiny.

In their childhood home, the old comfort between them rose up like a dazzling mist, and for a moment she almost forgot that Teri was dying.

Teri was why she was having the baby. Their parents only had the two of them, and their mother had always said, "We only had two, to replace each other. Any more than that is selfish." Ava knew she couldn't replace Teri, but at least she could light a little candle in the face of it. Her life had been a series of crashes, of hit-and-run accidents. She wanted to try to make one soft landing.

"It's not like your life's been a bump-free ride, but you seem to smooth out the bumps, as if you have superhuman shock absorbers," Ava said.

"Ava, I'm dying," Teri said, welling up with tears. "There's no shock absorbers for that."

"Oh, Ter, I'm sorry," Ava said, awkwardly bending over to hug her. "I mean . . ."

"It's okay. Just don't crush me to death," Teri said.

Ava rose as quickly as she could. The weight of the baby seemed to make every movement a slow, stretched blur, as if she were stoned.

Teri put her hand on Ava's belly. Ava couldn't help thinking it was the hand of death. She'd come home, she realized, at least in part to look for comfort herself. She had not really taken in the full weight of Teri's dying until now. Her illness and treatments had been stretching out for years, and both Ava and her mother had been able to pretend it might go on for years longer—until Teri moved back home, barely able to cross the room without help.

Ava remembered many times as a child running home in a fright and slamming the door behind her with a sense of total relief. Whatever was *out there* was not getting in. But it was inside now. Inside every room of every place she entered. Inside herself.

■　■　■

Robin was out "running." Though she knew about his affair, they had slipped back into the illusion. He claimed he was still going to run the marathon. Ava was so inside herself and the pregnancy that she was turning numb to the whole thing. She knew she wasn't going anywhere anytime soon. Reclining in the bathtub, she thought about the physical movement and change inside her. She was falling in love with her own body again. She stroked her tender breasts and slid her hands over her firm roundness. Floating, endless floating. With Robin's prodding, she had briefly entertained the idea of adoption. But now that the baby was stirring and Teri was fading, it was impossible.

Ava recalled her trips to abortion clinics—glum, sterile affairs. The kindly staff, the hushed tones. She had sworn after the last time, she'd never do it again. The truth was that she'd always been a bit careless about birth control. But her dancing days were over now.

It takes two to tango, it takes two to tangle, she sang to herself.

When Robin returned that evening, he moved jerkily around their condo, as if on speed. She was lying on the couch. His rapid pacing was making her nervous, too.

"What's up?" she asked, opening her eyes.

"Listen, Ava, we have to talk. Now, don't get upset. It's just that I've seen a lawyer. He's drawing up an agreement for us. To insure that you and the child are taken care of, that's all."

"For you to protect you from yourself? I don't get it."

"It's just so . . . we don't know what's going to happen . . . it's just so we all understand each other."

"Then why didn't we *all* meet with the lawyer?"

"See, you're making this adversarial already!"

"Adversarial? That's a lawyer word!" she shouted, plodding heavily out of the living room and into the baby's room, now cluttered with boxes. Robin had bought some tools, and they lay scattered on the floor. She curled up in a corner and sobbed.

"He wants a paternity test," he said through the closed door.

"I'll give you a fucking paternity test!" she shouted with vague menace. She meant castration, or something like it.

■　■　■

Ava never saw the Big Fucking Bird, even when it got warm enough to sit out on the deck on gentle spring afternoons. The wooden slats of the deck still smelled fresh, newly cut. When she walked over to the tree one day to get a closer look, her feet sinking into the wet, spongy grass, she saw a big orange X spray-painted on the other side of the tree. It was meant to come down—they were making room for a couple more condos. Inevitable. Like Baby X.

When she was dancing, putting herself on display, nothing penetrated, nobody got inside her. The dirty smudges of men's faces shouting at her. Oh, it was upscale, all right—men used to getting what they wanted. Each night after work, Ava drove home on random streets, making sure she wasn't being followed, a pile of soiled, folded bills spilled on the seat beside her. Once Robin asked her to dance for him. "Like you used to," he'd said. She tried, but she felt shamed and exposed in their quiet, brightly lit apartment. "I can't," she said. "It was a job. This isn't a job."

Robin accepted that. He understood about jobs.

■ ■ ■

Ava was startled one evening in late April when Robin asked her to watch him run in the marathon.

"You're actually going through with this?"

"She bailed on me when I told her about the baby situation."

"Sounds familiar." Her voice stiffened. "So that's my fault?"

"I told you it was no big deal."

"You think you can make it?"

"I can try. But I don't know anybody here to cheer me on."

"But why?" Ava wanted someone to cheer *her* on.

"Because it's there," he said, and forced a laugh.

She almost said something mean, but she was tired of mean things. "Okay, I'll go," she said. The truth didn't quite matter anymore. The only truth she could hold on to was that she was having a baby.

■ ■ ■

There were no hills in Rochester Hills. The "Hills" part was added so that the residents could feel superior to those in Rochester, the previous trendy suburb. There were no hills in the entire Detroit area, unless you counted the freeway overpasses. The marathon ran through the heart of Detroit—the old sick heart. The morning of the race was brisk and cool. Perfect for runners and pregnant women. Ava felt good to be out in it, her window rolled down. She took Woodward Avenue, one of the old main arteries of the city, rather than the freeway. She cruised over the wide, empty expanses of roadway—Sunday morning, the streets nearly deserted. A curious exhilaration rushed into her, carried by the cool wind.

A map of the race route sat on the seat next to her. She chose a spot the newspaper had mentioned as a good one, at the twenty-mile mark, under the clock of the old abandoned Hudson's department store, a mile before the runners crossed the bridge toward the finish line in Canada. She'd never been across the border before, and she wasn't sure Robin would make it that far, either.

■ ■ ■

The first three runners, all Kenyans, the prerace favorites, surged past her. Their thin, sinewy bodies carried a light sheen as the early sun hit them. They looked like they could run forever. They were the chosen ones, the ones who drifted effortlessly across the sea.

As each clump of runners passed in their wake, Ava noticed less grace, more struggle. The line between the elite runners and the amateurs was crossed in a mix of inconsistent gaits, out-and-out limps, ragged breathing, and red, sweaty faces. Where had all these vulnerable human bodies come from? Ava had rarely seen any runners during their months living there.

Her back ached, and her legs were rubbery. She pushed through to the street and asked some children to squeeze together so she could sit on the curb, though she wasn't sure she could stoop down without falling, or that if once down she'd ever be able to get up. The children's mother, standing above them, nudged them with her foot and smiled at Ava, putting a hand on her shoulder as she slowly lowered herself. Ava was briefly startled at the woman's touch. After she settled between the children, she looked up and smiled. "Thanks."

The woman nudged her children again. "You're welcome," they said in sing-song unison.

Still no sign of Robin. Some runners were reduced to walking. Others simply drifted off into the crowd, or disconsolately sat on the curb, uncertain of their next move. A man in top hat and tails limped past, his runner's number dangling from the back of his jacket.

"Cute don't cut it when you got twenty-six miles to run," the woman said.

"Do you think all these runners are from Detroit?" Ava asked.

"Who knows. We've only got sprinters in our neighborhood, eh, kids?" Her children ignored her, but she continued. "I don't want to see any of you sprinting down the street, some police car offering to give you a lift."

Her oldest daughter, perhaps fifteen, grunted and shuffled her feet.

"Is this your first?" the woman asked.

"My first marathon? Yes. My—my husband's running, though I haven't spotted him yet."

"Your first child. Is this your first *child?*" The woman shook her head at Ava like she was crazy.

"Oh, yes. Yes," Ava said, laughing. "I don't get out much. I don't know anybody here. No one ever asks me anything."

"Hon, you need to get yourself some maternity clothes," the woman said.

Ava was dressed in loose sweat pants and one of Robin's dress shirts. She was woozy, and the day was heating up. "Thanks for the tip," she said. "I went to Babyland last week."

"You need to go get something for your own self," the woman said. "Feel good about yourself."

Ava was the middle child, between Teri and Ted, her older brother, a disgraced priest no one had heard from in years. Her mother was busy nursing Teri. Robin was busy running somewhere in that mass of passing bodies. Ava never felt more alone.

"Is *your* husband running?" she asked, squinting up at the woman, who snorted and laughed so loudly that Ava thought she might be choking. She nudged her children with her foot again.

"Hey, kids, this lady wants to know is your father running the race?"

That provoked an even more raucous response from the children.

"Your husband gonna need his strength for when that baby comes. What's he doing in this crazy race? This is one of the few days it's safe to be out here."

"That ain't true," her oldest son said flatly.

"Not true? I can't even go to the corner to get me a gallon of milk." She smacked the back of his head. "Not true, ha."

"Are these all yours?" Ava asked.

"All five of them." The woman laughed. "Knuckleheads every one of them. Now, don't get me wrong, kids are great. Right, kids?" She kicked the oldest boy with her toe.

"Ma, cut that shit out, will ya?" he said.

Ignoring him, the woman turned back to Ava. "Seen your husband yet?" They were down to the last small clumps. The sparse crowd was drifting away. The last remaining stragglers were struggling to finish, to avoid the humiliation of dropping out. But they had six more miles to go, and it wasn't looking good. Ava realized that she'd stopped looking for Robin a long time ago.

"I don't know." She shrugged. Perhaps he'd already snuck by and was in Canada applying for political asylum, a refugee from fatherhood. "I guess I'll just go home now."

"That's good, hon," the woman said, pulling Ava to her feet, then patting her hand. "Don't worry. You're gonna be all right." The woman had three balloons tied to her wrist, and they bounced against her whenever she gestured. "Now, you go find that man of yours."

"Maybe he dropped out." Ava shrugged. The children were hunched over, playing with pebbles at the edge of the curb. She was struck by their thin exposed necks, like the stems of fragile flowers. Or weeds. She'd have one of her own soon. The broken clock loomed above her, quietly casting its circle of shade onto the street like a reverse spotlight. She slowly walked away in the direction of her car. Like the last of the runners, she was in no hurry.

Bouncy Castle

"Show us your tits!" the neatly lettered sign read. **Someone had** clearly planned ahead for this debauchery—as opposed to the more spontaneous kinds of debauchery that were going on all around us on the infield at the Kentucky Derby.

I'd never said that to anyone in my life. In the outside world, it'd get you slapped, punched, fired, kicked out. Sure, I think it from time to time, but I have never put it quite that way to any of my girlfriends or my ex-wife, and certainly not to her, Sara (no h). Being polite, I might say something like, "Yes, from the outside you appear to have a very attractive figure, and I would be very pleased to see your breasts uncovered." Though I'd never expressed it in those terms, either.

Sara's breasts, in fact, sagged a bit. She was pushing forty. I'd hit the magic number myself, so this is meant as no criticism. We get old, our bodies start flapping around any which way, everything loosening up for the home stretch. The first time I noticed it, I was bent over, picking up a dropped sock, and caught myself in the full-length mirror in the hallway outside my bathroom. This loose, flabby thing hung down—it was my belly. It looked like something you could just lop off like a piece of fat off a steak. No muscle tone. Who has time for that? I ask you. It's hard enough to maintain any kind of tone in daily life, struggling against the off-key, the bitter, the grating and grinding, the sudden stops, the circling back. Don't use that tone of voice with me! When I stood up, the sag pretty much disappeared, but I knew it was there. And that it didn't used to be there.

Don't! *Don't* show me your tits! Show me the big toe on your left foot. Show me the warm, wet skin behind your knee. Show me your crooked teeth and jeweled spit.

■ ■ ■

Sara and I had met at one of these hokey singles clubs. They were really getting specialized—this one had a group called "First-time Losers, Second-time Winners?" for divorced people forty and under. Stu, the guy who ran the larger umbrella organization, "Detroit's Successful Singles," had once been a poet of some renown who'd had a poem about snowflakes published in the *New Yorker.* He told everybody that when they met him. Despite that achievement, he'd been lonely and an alcoholic, so the bar scene was off limits. He started with a coed singles volleyball league, and that was still a staple of the organization. Every year, he'd have a tournament with a team from each of his singles groups competing. Stu had been divorced twice since starting Detroit's Successful Singles, and he even made that part of his shtick: no guarantees.

After my divorce, I'd debated the whole hair thing. Mine's all gray and turning white, which adds a few years to my looks. It's the first thing women seem to notice. Should I dye it? Should I wear a sign that says I'm really only forty though I look fifty? My bald friend Cliff even dyes the C clamp of hair around his bald head. Divorce. Desperation is the name of the game. With a capital D and

that rhymes with T and that stands for Trouble. I'd tried the dye
job once, but I hated the smell, and it looked completely phony. I
looked like a sixty-year-old guy dyeing his hair to look fifty, so it
added yet another ten years to my life. I dyed it on a Friday night,
then desperately searched for a hair salon to dye it back to gray
the next day. "Smart move," the stylist said.

Specifically, Sara and I met at the inflatable bouncy thing Stu
had set up as part of the getting acquainted picnic. The idea was
to make us feel silly, I guess. Like kids. Let your guard down and
all that. I saw one guy fall and ruin his comb-over. He quickly tried
to get up and pat everything down in place again, but it was hopeless—he was done for the night. He looked like a sad, lopsided bear
lumbering out of the plastic entrance. This young peppy woman
kept trying to nudge me into the Bouncy Castle.

"I'll just watch," I said.

"That's not playing fair," the young woman scolded with a condescending grin.

"What's fair got to do with it?" Sara interrupted. She'd been
about ten feet away, but Peppy Preppy's voice carried pretty far. I
wondered if she was one of Stu's ringers. Stu denied using ringers,
though none of us believed him—she was *too* young, *too* peppy.

"You two seem well matched," Peppy said sarcastically, and
wandered off.

Sara was smoking. "I don't usually smoke," she said immediately.
"Do you think the Bouncy Castle will blow up if I drop an ash in
it?" She flicked her cigarette close to the outside edge.

"I think it'll just melt."

"Too bad. I can just see the headline: Divorcée Blows Up Bouncy
Castle, 30 Losers Lost."

"Wait, we're second-time *winners,* remember?"

"I've been divorced twice. I snuck in." She laughed. "By the way,
how old are you?"

"Forty. Want to see my birth certificate?"

"Don't get defensive on me now," she said, squeezing my hand. "Sara. Thirty-seven."

"Donald," I said. I squeezed back, then let go.

It turned out that technically she hadn't been divorced twice. She'd had a live-in for a few years that didn't work out, and she counted that.

I'd never liked people who were all over you physically like that, no sense of personal space, but after I got divorced and had all the personal space I wanted, I welcomed the occasional invasion of warm skin against my own—even accidental brushes in the grocery store line. I found myself living for those.

We wandered together across the picnic area Stu had reserved. They also had one of those wretched pits with a thousand colored balls in it.

"They should have everybody take their clothes off before they climb in," she said. "It'd make things more interesting."

"Somebody'd get hurt," I said.

"Somebody always gets hurt," she said. "That's part of the deal."

"Not for me, it isn't," I said warily. She was an attractive blonde who fit nicely into her tight jeans. "Looks like a McDonald's playground. Maybe we can get Happy Meals," I said.

"You got kids?" she asked.

"You're breaking all the rules," I said. The Bible according to Stu said not to mention kids until the second meeting.

"Stu's full of shit. Everybody knows that. He's like the rich kid who has the pool when you're growing up—you hang around by the fence and try to be her friend during the summer so she'll invite you in."

"I was the kid with the pool," I said. "But I never invited anybody in until they invited me to their house first."

"You showed them."

"Then somebody else got a pool."

"Somebody else always gets a pool."

"That's why I don't dye my hair."

"Well, that's a start. Do I have to invite you to my house first?"

"I don't have any kids."

"Me, neither. I borrow my sister's once in a while but always return them promptly."

"Kids are all right," I said. I'd always wanted children, but Shirley, my ex, never felt things were stable enough between us, and she was right. "As long as they're locked up in Bouncy Castles."

She smiled, and I noticed her crooked teeth. I'd been seeing way too many adults with braces, so I suddenly wanted to kiss her. Once you're out of your teens, straight teeth isn't going to be a make-or-break issue. Is it?

■ ■ ■

"When they fall out, I'll get some straight ones," Sara said once when we were in bed together.

"You don't hear me complaining, do you?" I said. First time around, I'd tried to change my wife. I nagged her to death. Well, not to death. To Scottsdale, Arizona, with her cousin's ex-husband.

A lot of marriages split up because somebody's having an affair, so the other person usually gets the sympathy vote. In my case, that would be me. But in a group like the two-timers, most people knew in their hearts it was more complicated than that. All those clear words usually got all smeary, even before somebody started screwing around. The newly divorced, angry ones who wanted martyr status were shunned by the rest of us. They should've had their own group, the "Call Me in Six Months" group.

I drove trucks for the Bray's Belly Buster restaurant chain. Our symbol was a laughing donkey holding a burger and fries in his hands. Or paws. Or hooves—whatever the hell you want to call them. Everything I wore had a laughing donkey on it. The Bray's donkey was a disgusting creature. Few families ever entered the realm of the donkey. Some families got takeout, but most Bray's had no tables—they were designed so you either sat along the outside windows on a long, thin, stainless steel counter looking out onto the street, or you ate at the semicircular counter surrounding the grill. Cheap, simple, no frills. The square, frozen burger patties, which I had to unload from my refrigerated truck, had tiny holes stamped in them. They smothered the meat in fried onions, and if you ate too many of them, you did indeed have a Bray's Belly Buster. The restaurants stayed open all night and did a good business after the bars closed. In fact, the company researchers tried to place them within a mile of at least a half dozen bars. I worked odd shifts with long hours, and that made it easy for Shirley to get on the express to Scottsdale. If I'd been working nine to five, we might've lasted five more unhappy years together.

Sara was a manager at El Chico's, one of those fake Mexican restaurants that specialized in fried ice cream. The whole staff had to come out and sing some fake Mexican birthday song whenever it was a customer's birthday. So we both had jobs that made us look like asses in more explicit ways than most jobs.

Stu's gigs weren't cheap. He had you fill out these forms when you applied. I didn't want to know his criteria. I never met anyone unemployed at any of those things, though it was clear that Sara and I weren't on the rich side of the teeter-totter.

■　■　■

Nearby, two men were arguing loudly at the volleyball net. The uniformed, cute-T-shirted staff closed in and broke things up, but it definitely put a damper on the evening. We weren't kids anymore, and two grown men nearly coming to blows over a stupid volleyball game made us all seem like the first-time losers that we were.

"I think they got off at the wrong picnic. Anger management's the next picnic shelter down," Sara said.

"What's the point in being so cynical?" I said as we wandered off toward the parking lot. "After all, you're here, aren't you?"

She sighed. "No, I'm *not* here, Donald."

Her calling me Donald like that, sounding so defeated and wistful—I fell in love with her just then. Wasps circled a garbage can full of watermelon rinds. All of our sad teeth marks on display, our messy, uneven mouths unable to get all the red stuff. And we wanted all the sweet, juicy red stuff. All our lives we'd wanted it. That's why we were there.

■ ■ ■

We both loved horse racing, and the Hazel Park Raceway was nearly halfway between our apartments. We started meeting there after work to place our bets. I bet conservative and often came out slightly ahead. For a while, I just bet on every horse Dave Vallone rode, and I did quite well, but then Dave left town to ride at Belmont, and I never found a jockey that hot again. I loved the thoroughbreds, their desperate lunging. I couldn't stand the trotters, though—their manufactured, imposed gait just made me more conscious of how we were all shaped by the almighty dollar. Sometimes, getting stiffly down out of the truck, I knew how it felt to have your step altered by the quest for money. We skipped harness racing season altogether. Even their name—trotters—implied something distasteful to me.

Sara, she won or lost big. She liked betting on anything. She'd even speculate on how long we'd last together. We went from one month to six, and she kept handicapping us till suddenly we were going on a year, and all bets were off.

We'd never been anywhere together, so for our one-year anni-versary, we planned a trip to the Kentucky Derby.

"Donald, let's get one of those kinky honeymoon rooms with a hot tub," she said one night. We were practically living together then, though I still kept my own place. We were both a little leery of jumping into the same address, though sometimes we talked of buying a house together. It turned out that we'd both had surgery to ensure that we'd never have kids. "Double protection," I said. "That's what I like." It was another sign that we were fated to be together.

Fate and good sex. What more could I ask for? I'd had my vasectomy on my fortieth birthday. I didn't want to be an old daddy—it was one less thing to worry about. But then I didn't have sex with anyone for the next six months—until I met Sara—so I'd thought I'd jinxed myself.

Actually, they had requested proof of age for the First-time Losers Club. So many people had been lying about their age that they'd hardly had anybody left in the forty-to-fifty age group, the Second-Wind Club. I called to make sure it was forty and under, not under forty. I had six months left when I joined, so I wanted to meet somebody fast. Somebody younger who filled a pair of jeans like Sara.

■　■　■

We made our reservations for Louisville and headed down I-75 in my pickup on the first Friday in May. We got our Jacuzzi room on the outskirts of the city near X-stasy, a large adult "films, novelties, and live dancers" place where the gravel parking lot was littered with large rigs parked in awkward rows.

"Ever been in one of those places?" Sara asked.

I paused. "Sure. When I was younger. Life on the road, you know. Cheap thrills . . ." Our hotel was a Hampton Court, a national chain of semibudget places, on the edge of the fast-food wonderland that bled from nearly every other exit off any freeway in America. "But the thrills were too cheap—it was depressing. What a way to make a living, having guys stare at your body. I mean, how would that make you feel after a while?"

"I don't know," she said. "Singing 'Happy Birthday' in fake Spanish is no big thrill, either, and it pays less."

"How do you know?"

"Listen, Donald, anything involving sex has to cost more than anything involving food."

"You think?"

"For people like us, anyway. How come so many of your sentences start with 'When I was younger'?"

"It'd be hard to start them with 'When I was older,'" I grumbled.

"Sounds like somebody needs a Happy Meal," she teased. She was in an excited, playful mood. She seemed freer and more relaxed in a way that unnerved me a little.

"We're too old for Happy Meals," I said. "Twelve and under."

"They should have grown-up Happy Meals with little sex toys inside."

"You want 'em, I bet X-stasy's got 'em."

"How often did you and Shirley do it?"

"How often did you and Posie do it? How could you marry someone named Posie?"

"It was a nickname. You mean at the beginning or at the end?"

"In the middle."

"Every other day and twice on weekends."

"I was on the road a lot," was all I said about Shirley, and Sara let it pass.

Sara and I had sex with what Shirley would have thought was alarming regularity. She almost demanded it, getting me hard with confident stroking, kissing, even when I came home exhausted and smelling of diesel fuel and fried meat. Nights after the track were incredible, whether we won or lost. We were both pumped up, ready to act after all the watching, ready to stretch and lunge.

■ ■ ■

The Hampton Court had no court. We pulled up in front of our room, threw our bags on the floor, popped a bottle of champagne, and filled up the Jacuzzi tub. The Jacuzzi was on a slightly raised platform next to the bathroom in a large tiled area surrounded by mirrors.

Sara did a playful striptease and slipped into the water. I felt like a goofball, but I did the same. I set the champagne bottle on the edge of the tub. The jets were slamming water into my lower back. I moved a bit to the side and squeezed next to Sara. The tub was more of a one-and-a-half-person tub, and our bodies clumsily came together, half in and half out of the water. I'd forgotten to turn the lights off. Not that I needed them off, but I'd left them all on, including the big glaring overhead. Whoever designed the Honeymoon Hideaway room hadn't given lighting much thought. I suppose candles would have been nice, but we hadn't brought our own. They weren't something I usually packed in my overnight trucker duffle.

I felt like it was New Year's Eve, a holiday I hated—all that pressure to have fun, no way to live up to the buildup. Sara, she was squealing and playful and splashing and on top of me. The hot water seemed to make my entire body flaccid, and no matter what Sara tried, I wasn't getting up for the occasion.

"C'mon, Donald, what's the deal? This isn't like you. What do you want me to do?"

I picked up the thread of restrained irritation in her voice and sewed myself into a corner. "It's no big deal," I said. "Is it?"

"You giving up for the night?"

"Let's get into the bed. Maybe we're not the hot-tub type."

"Well, maybe somebody isn't," she said. "What happened to my macho trucker dude?"

"Gee, thanks, you're doing wonders for my confidence," I said. "Don't start on the trucker thing, either. I hate that shit."

"So much for that," Sara said finally. She stood from the tub and, dripping water onto the thin indoor/outdoor carpeting, walked to the window and peeked out the curtains.

I got out and dried myself off. They did have nice, thick towels. And a sign that said you could *buy* the towels, and the Hampton Court champagne glasses. And if they were missing when you left, that meant you *were* buying them.

I thought about walking up and putting my arms around her from behind, but the bed was a king, and it lured me down onto its enormous surface. My skin was wrinkled yet spongy from the Jacuzzi. The water'd been too hot, and the pressure on, and there was just no comfortable way to do it in there, I told myself. It was too small.

"What are you looking at?"

"The outside," she said. I had no idea what that meant. I slipped under the covers and, despite my plan to wait her out and make deep, passionate love to her when she finally came to bed, immediately fell into a deep sleep.

■　■　■

The next thing I knew, our wake-up call was jangling through my head, and I was staring up at the mirrored ceiling. Sara's eyes met mine in the mirror.

"Sorry," I said.

"Me, too," she said. That seemed ambiguous, but I groggily shook it off.

"Remember the June Taylor Dancers?" I asked, and started waving my arms and legs into star-shaped patterns.

"No," Sara said, but she started mimicking my movements. We looked pretty good up there, synchronized, kaleidoscopic, our flesh flattened against us, and I thought the day might be a good one after all.

The infield gates opened at six A.M. Sara wanted to be there early to get a spot where we could see the horses. She slapped my butt, and I stumbled out of bed. She dressed in a sexy blue halter top with jeans, and a jean jacket on top of that, for it was still cool out as we stepped into the quiet parking lot, the *whoosh* of cars from the interstate a constant breeze. After a decent breakfast at LuAnne's, we were both recharged with the excitement of the day to come. LuAnne's was a truck stop that had been recommended to me by Gino Martucci, the Bray's driver for southern Ohio and Kentucky. Gino was a boy who could clear his plate, and I could see how LuAnne's would appeal to him. Huge portions, grease floating through the air, seeping into your pores.

I wore my usual jeans and a plain T-shirt. At first, I used to get a kick (no pun intended) out of the donkey on my shirt, but it was too close to the "Donald" in script, and I didn't want people linking us. We picked up half-pints of bourbon from an enterprising young man who was selling them out of a cardboard box in the parking lot—easy to slip in past the guards. They didn't care if you got drunk—they just wanted you to drink their watery beer and exorbitantly priced sickly-sweet mint juleps at the cinder-block concession stands inside.

"I'm starting to feel a little old," I said to Sara as we waited in line to enter. "Don't look now, but we're surrounded by teenaged misfits."

"Relax," Sara said. "It's got to be better than another one of Stu's scripted parties."

"I don't know. I kind of feel like I could use a script," I said as we witnessed the first vomiting of the day. Sara and I had finished the rest of the flat champagne in the hotel that morning before LuAnne's. Maybe because we'd paid for it, and it was there. Or maybe we wanted to be a little reckless. Or maybe we wanted to wash away the lingering disappointment from the night before.

Once inside the gates, we tried to get as close to the track as we could but were dismayed to find that the infield fence was well inside the track's inside rail, so even there, the horses were going to be far away. We thought we could at least catch glimpses of the races, but the rush and tangle of young bodies filled in the space between us and the fence, displacing other people's blankets, or overlapping them, or simply standing on them, so that by the time the first race started, we could see nothing except a mass of drunken bodies. No way to see which horse won—you had to listen to the loudspeakers and trust their call. No one in the infield seemed to mind.

The half-pints were gone by noon. We'd neglected to pack anything to eat, and neither of us typically drank the hard stuff. Which was one of the reasons Stu's group appealed to us—he didn't allow drinking at his events. So, we were loaded and dizzy in the heat by the time I finally got to the front of the food line and got us some pitiful french fries and hot dogs, and we wolfed them down.

I kept looking for other people with gray hair. There were some shaved heads, but the only gray I saw was on a stoned-out old white dude with Rastafarian braids who looked as though he hadn't bathed since the death of Bob Marley more than twenty years ago.

We didn't know quite what to do with ourselves. At the Hazel Park track, we sat in the grandstand, and we were always focused on the races—horses, jockeys, bets.

"Isn't this wild?" Sara kept saying. Outrageous behavior ruled the day. Guzzling contests. Streaking. Dancing in a pit of mud to bass-driven boom boxes that were somehow allowed inside. And lots of topless women. Some guys nearby held up a sign, "Show Us Your Tits for $5," though after a few takers, they ripped off the part that said "for $5" and simply became more enthusiastic and encouraging in their drunkenness. Whenever a young woman suc-cumbed, we'd hear a huge roar of whistles and shouts and turned our heads to look. Those roars were the bestial punctuation for that long, hot day.

"I'm not going to take my shirt off," I joked with Sara. Not around all those young, hard, reckless bodies. "I don't want to show off and make all these young kids jealous." I could have fathered a son old enough to be one of those young bucks posturing with their muscles and tattoos in front of the trashed, crowded bathrooms on the infield.

I knew we should've tried to get grandstand seats, but Sara had insisted on the infield. "I've spent too much time in the fancy seats," she said, "and look where it's got me."

When we sat on our blanket—an old patchwork quilt my Aunt Marie had made—I felt diminished. Everyone else around us stood, so finally, we stood, too, then my back began to ache from standing. Our muddy shoes marked up Aunt Marie's beautiful old quilt until it was no longer fit to sit on.

"Can we leave now?" I asked, four races into the day. I couldn't imagine six more. The Derby was the eighth race. Saying that was a mistake, but I wanted to leave.

"You're kidding, right?" she asked. But she knew I wasn't, and there was no reason to answer.

"Why should we stay? Let's go back to the motel." I was eager to nap, then try again in air-conditioned peace and quiet. To hell with the Jacuzzi.

"And do what, lie around and watch bad TV?" she said.

"Why don't we? *This* is bad TV," I said, gesturing around me as another roar erupted on cue from the "Tits Pit," as I heard some pimply-faced goon refer to it.

"Donald, you disappoint me," she said. "I think you're ready for the Second Winders."

I wished she was smiling when she said that, but no such luck. "Low blow," I said, smiling anyway, embarrassed.

"I'll give you a low blow," she said, smiling back and miming a knee to the groin. If only that had been the real low blow. She promptly turned her back on me and pushed her way through to the—I can't even call it that again—the breast-revealing area. And, not knowing what to do, I chased after her. When I reached her and began pulling on her arm, she shouted, "Let go!" and some helpful young men detached her from me, and she sashayed up in front of the sign and lifted her halter, then turned to face the other direction and lifted her top again to hoots and hollers, to the delight of the masses. I shrank to my knees in disbelief and disgust. My heart shriveled up into a wilted mint julep leaf.

"We don't know anybody here," Sara insisted truthfully and loudly as she came back to me, still aware of the surrounding audience, as I was. "Why is it such a big deal?" Her tongue was thick in her mouth, and her voice had the raw, silly lilt of someone over the hump of drunkenness and headed toward Hangoversville. "We don't know anyone here!" she screamed at me, and somebody said, "Right on, babe! You tell 'em."

I was wasted, too. No one should get up at five A.M. and start drinking. Even the high school and college students shouldn't do it. Getting drunk that early alters your day so dramatically that there's no time to recover. Not without a good nap, anyway, and though I stepped over many passed-out bodies on dirty blankets that afternoon, I don't think anyone would've called that napping—too much vomit in close proximity.

I wanted a shower. I wanted to be clean. I wanted Sara to be clean. I wanted warm water to rain down on us. I wanted to lie on cool sheets in air-conditioned bliss with the remote control and randomly flip the channels while Sara laid her wet hair against my chest.

I ran away from her, dancing clumsily over the muddy blankets till I reached the high fence around the infield. We were like contained prisoners, allowed to riot while the grandstanders actually watched the races. I finally reached the gate and pushed my way out between a couple of overweight, well-dressed tourists from Mars who seemed to be studying the grandstand crowd with their binoculars.

■　■　■

"How could you abandon me there, run away from me when I'm talking to you? That's so immature."

We were eating biscuits and gravy at LuAnne's—again. We had finally met each other at the truck. And finding it had been quite a chore for both of us. There were few vehicles left in the dusty, rutted parking lot, and mine was one of them. When I got there, I found Sara sprawled forlornly on the hood.

"We shouldn't be talking maturity here, Sara," I said, smacking my napkin across my face.

"Why not?"

I lowered my voice. "Showing your breasts to a bunch of—a bunch of boys—doesn't rate very high on the maturity scale."

"Oh, just chill out, will you? Why are you such a prude all of a sudden? It's like that Jacuzzi baptized you into some weird religious cult or something."

I winced. What would that be, the cult of Can't Get It Up? "C'mon, Sara," I said. "I'm sorry for freaking out on you. We were both drunk. Let's forget about it. This whole thing was a bad idea."

"What?" Her voice broke. "What whole thing?"

"I mean coming down here."

"You wouldn't think it'd be a bad idea to go on a trip to celebrate being together a year. What are the odds of that?"

"Don't go placing any bets. Can't we just move on?"

"What?"

"Move on from this and back to where we were."

Don't show me your tits! Show me the big toe on your left foot. Show me the warm, wet skin behind your knee. Show me your crooked teeth and jeweled spit. I was worried that every time I saw her breasts from then on, I'd see those drunken, red-faced boys leering at them, but it turned out I needn't have worried, for I never saw her breasts again.

"You're a two-time loser," she said. Name-calling, I think that violated another one of Stu's rules. "Are you going to run away on me again when something happens that you don't like?"

"I just wanted to see the horses," I said lamely. I was stuffing my face, but I wasn't the least bit hungry.

■　■　■

Not that there were many pretty sights during the races, but afterward, thousands of fried human beings stumbling out the gates was enormously ugly and sad and had little to do with the beauty of horse racing. We'd bought special Kentucky Derby mint julep glasses but then left them somewhere in the piles of trash that littered the infield. It looked like a small war had been fought with garbage as weapons—cans, paper, bottles, busted-up coolers, clothes, blankets, and probably a few teeth and handfuls of hair as well, based on the number of brawls that seemed to spill aimlessly across the rough sea of blankets during the course of the morning and afternoon, peaking in late afternoon as the shadows lengthened and people got colder, number, and sadder. Aunt Marie's blanket was in one of those piles.

After that hot May Saturday, rain came on Sunday. As I drove north, it crashed into the windshield of my Bronco, relentless. Visibility obscured. I had paid for the hotel, so Sara insisted on buying breakfast—and gas, when we filled up outside Cincinnati. She was using the cash from her winnings, her only souvenir quickly disappearing. On the first race, I had bet a favorite to show and made forty cents on my two dollars. Sara picked the winner, ten-to-one odds, on her twenty-dollar bet and picked up two hundred, though she lost every other race she'd managed to bet on before we got too shit-faced, before we got swallowed up in the infield and forgot completely that every so often a dizzying rush of horses was passing by somewhere in the distance.

Everybody needed somebody to blame, and I blamed Sara. Blamed her for being the kind of person that attracted me in the first place. And on that long ride home, I couldn't stop myself from blaming her, from stewing in the silence of my own making as she slowly made up her mind to be rid of me.

There's not much of roadside Ohio worth mentioning, but Sara dutifully commented on every cow, every brightly painted barn, every odd license plate. I drove for a living and found none of it interesting. Every day, I drove from here to there, from there to here. I worried about the truck. I worried about making good time. I listened to books on tape and forgot, vigorously forgot, that I was delivering gray square patties of frozen meat throughout the Midwest.

But now I was on a different route. Forgetting anything was impossible. I'd apologized, and I realized that she hadn't. I thought she needed to apologize. I was keeping score like some old married guy, I realize now, all that personal space surrounding me once again.

When I dropped her off at her place, she didn't invite me in. When I called the next day, she didn't answer. The next day, all the stuff I kept at her place was piled neatly in two paper bags outside the door of my building, with "DONALD" in all caps scrawled with a Sharpie marker across them.

■ ■ ■

Stu had mixed feelings about the successful unions formed at his outings, for it meant two fewer customers. It may have been why he himself kept becoming single again—he seemed addicted to the game. The odd posturing and bluffing, the hesitations and missteps. He was both voyeur and participant. He always seemed quite chummy with his pert little assistants, who, unlike Stu, never seemed to get any older. Stu liked to think of himself as the Dick Clark of the local singles scene. He'd had work done, you could tell. And his skin always had the odd orange tint of the tanning salon.

He was clearly happy to see me, to shake my trembling hand when I walked into his tiny office above the Personality hair salon on Forbes across from the Squirrel Cage, his favorite haunt back in his drinking days.

"Donald," he said. "Welcome back." He held up his hands as if to say, "I don't want to know," and it was clear he didn't. The fact that I was there without Sara was enough for him. He offered me some fluorescent green power drink from the small fridge next to his desk and pulled out my file. He stared at it for longer than I thought he needed to. What information could he be studying?

"Still driving for Bray's?" he asked finally.

"Hee-haw," I said glumly.

"Donald, you just had a birthday, my man," he said, staring straight at me. "You know what that means?"

In retrospect, it seems impossible for me to have not thought of that before I stepped into his office.

Stu had his *New Yorker* poem framed on his wall. He got a lot of mileage out of that damned insipid poem. I had no idea what it was about. That's the kind of poem the *New Yorker* likes. You read it and say, "Hmmm," and go on to the next cartoon. Stu had the pool, and I was at the gate once again.

"Not the Second Winders." I moaned audibly. Stu claimed he was thirty-seven.

"Look, buddy, you can be a rookie all over again. The new kid in the age bracket. You'll have to beat them off with a stick."

"Stu, that's not an appealing image," I said.

"Some real babes in the Second Winders. I mean, talk about second wind—these women are hungry, Donald. They come from these dull, sexless marriages, and they're ready to rock 'n' roll. They're hungry, and you're a fresh piece of meat."

I don't look like the stereotypical trucker—the tattoos, the belly, the ball hat, the dirty jokes, etc.—but as soon as somebody finds out that's what I do, they start talking to me differently. Like I'm some crude, primitive being.

I was thinking about Sara. Maybe *crude*'s the wrong word. Isn't *unashamed* another word for *crude,* at least some of the time? And unashamed is a good thing, right? Sara would still be in the First-time Losers, and I wondered if she had returned to Stu as well. I knew better than to ask.

■ ■ ■

I couldn't believe they used the Bouncy Castle for the Second Winders, too. I guess Stu owned the damn thing, so he wanted to get his money's worth. Since I was starting over with a new group, I went out and got my hair dyed again. This time professionally. I had her leave some gray on the sides. A light rain fell, and it was a cool evening—late August, but it felt like September. And I tell you that to help explain why, when they parted the plastic flaps, I jumped in.

In a Cavern

The tour was even worse than Chuck had imagined. He and Sharmela were in the middle of Wolf Cave, the only natural cave in Michigan, being led around by Gus, their guide, a pimply-faced teenager with a flashlight. Vernon and Merlene—an elderly couple looking healthier than they had any right to—were the only others in their group. The only others in the whole cave, as far as Chuck could tell. He wanted to be back in the warm, pleasant sunshine of the first perfect day in what had been a rainy spring. He was used to heat, the ovens in his bakery churning it out in waves. The cave was cold and damp—like all caves were, he imagined. They hadn't brought jackets, having stopped at the cave on a whim after the winery in Paw Paw they'd planned on visiting was overrun by a bus full of tourists.

The bakery was doing great, and he'd suddenly become interested in houses, since it finally looked like they'd be able to buy one. He was a little cranky about missing out on the winery tour. Even Gus thought the winery was cool. It turned out that he'd applied for a job there, too, but "they only hire sweet old ladies."

"One of those sweet old ladies was pretty nasty to us," Chuck said. "She wouldn't let us join the tour. She said we had to make our own reservation. Just because."

"Too much of the world operates on 'just because,'" Vernon harrumphed. Vernon got by on harrumphs and dismissive snorts, mock outrage and exaggerated derision.

■　■　■

"Here you see Devil's Staircase," Gus said.

"Gus," Vernon Little began, "I think that looks more like an organ in an old cathedral. What do you think?"

"I never been in an old cathedral, Mister, so I couldn't say."

"Well, then, have you been in hell and *seen* the Devil's Staircase, and does it look like that?"

"Listen, Grandpa, I just say what they tell me to say. You want to lead the tour?"

"Grandpa? I could give you a spanking, you impudent, sniveling boy."

"Now, Vernon . . . " his wife, Merlene, said wearily.

Chuck and Sharmela looked at each other. He hadn't heard anyone say "impudent" in many years, if ever. Certainly not in the bakery.

The next stop was the Chapel of the Angels, an area Chuck thought was aptly named—enormous columns of rock in a semicircle around what could have been an altar. Or a shelf for the Big It, Chuck's name for his Supreme Being. "I'd like to walk through here on drugs," he said. That shut them all up. "I bet you'd see all kinds of things then," he continued uncertainly. Chuck still smoked a lot of pot, a source of contention with Sharmela, who had been attending Crossroads, a self-improvement center, twice a week with his brother Nate and coming home late. Something was fishy, and it wasn't Chuck's bread.

Sharmela whacked him in the ribs with her elbow, taking advantage of the dim light to give him a good one. He gasped. "Don't mind Charlie. Let's keep moving," Sharmela said. "Let Gus read his script, and we can imagine whatever we want."

"Chapel of the Angels? Give me a break," Vernon said, but he stepped in line and followed Merlene.

Sharmela seemed edgy. She clutched the iron railings of the cave staircases, even when paused for one of Gus's inane explanations. Chuck and Sharmela were both thirty-three. Chuck took a close look at Sharmela in the dim, eerie light. She had the look of a smoker—pale and thin—but she did not smoke. He was the smoker. That's one of the things he had always liked about her—you couldn't take anything at face value. She was always surprising him. Like the whole God thing. She'd spent a year studying to be a nun, though she referred to it now like a prison sentence she'd served and did not want to relive. The Crossroads thing had seemed like another surprise, something he half listened to at the dinner table after a long day at the bakery, but that channel wasn't changing, and Chuck wanted to find the clicker fast.

Chuck believed in a Supreme Being. Somebody to organize the whole thing. The Big It. The Big It must think it's all a real hoot—the outfits people wore to show what team they're on—every religion had them. Chuck had been raised a Catholic, and he thought they were the worst. Most nuns didn't wear those weird, heavy outfits anymore, but the priests still wore theirs. When he was an altar boy, Chuck had dutifully worn his cassock and surplice. Everything seemed designed to make you sweat. The Big It must've loved all the sweat shed in his name for no good reason. Chuck didn't believe in uniforms of any kind, and he made sure he got a job that did not require one—at least a formal one.

Though Chuck did like the idea of priests and rabbis wearing name tags in script over the breast. Maybe some kind of God logo. He thought it'd be nice if all religions had a common symbol for their Supreme Being. Allah/Jesus/God/Vishnu—whoever. The

Great Whoever. That way, everyone could acknowledge one common thing. One big common thing. Sharmela became an atheist just because some horny old nun came on to her when she was a novice. Horny people came on to other people and used power to their advantage in every walk of life and occupation in the world. That could go on the list of commonalities, too, Chuck thought. Supreme Being. Horniness. What else? Horniness didn't negate the existence of God, that's for sure. He hadn't asked Sharmela where sex figured in the Crossroads doctrine, but he knew it couldn't figure very high, since they hadn't made love in weeks. Maybe months. No God *or* sex. And he still couldn't figure out what they did have—it seemed to have something to do with making people talk about themselves with uncomfortable frankness.

■ ■ ■

"Chuck, you remember that flat tire I had last week?"

"Yeah." He hated when she called him Chuck—it meant something was up. When things were normal, she called him Charlie, just because no one else did. He was sure Vernon and Merlene and Gus could hear every word in the quiet, hollow, echoing cave.

"There wasn't no flat tire."

"*Any* flat tire," Vernon said under his breath.

"This can wait, Sharm," Chuck said flatly. This sounded like the beginning of the story that'd been in his head, the one he didn't want to ever hear. The others were all turned back toward them, waiting.

"No, it can't. I have to talk now. Maybe it's the cave . . . it's like a confessional."

Chuck winced. "We'll catch up, don't worry about us!" he shouted to the others. They hesitated. "Don't worry, Gus, old buddy, we'll tip you good. We won't deface anything. Promise."

Gus reluctantly turned forward again, leading the others. "Some people think this one looks like Abraham Lincoln. *You* might think it looks like Moses parting the Red Sea or a constipated giraffe . . ." He looked at Vernon.

"Gus is going to be all right without you," Chuck said to Sharmela when she seemed to hesitate.

"It does sort of remind me of a confessional," Merlene said, her voice wafting back to them as she disappeared in the darkness.

"Okay, let's have it," Chuck said.

"How long we been married now?" Sharmela asked.

"You figure it out," he said, trying to scuff his feet on the slimy cave floor without slipping. He rubbed his arms and shivered.

"How long?"

"Jesus Christ, let's get to the flat tire. The *un*-flat tire."

"Ten years. I think ten years is a nice round number. Round numbers allow you to change."

"I think eleven looks nice, too, two stick people standing together. What you getting at?"

"Well, if you're married ten years and get divorced, nobody can say you didn't give it a good try."

"I'm going to catch up to Gus," Chuck said, and turned quickly away from her, heading down the narrow, dim-lit path. Ten good years, he thought. Things had been, what?—unexciting?—for the past couple of years, but that happened to everybody. He didn't think *he* was unhappy. Somewhere between unexcited and unhappy, and he'd been worse places. He had a pain in his side that told him Sharmela had not only betrayed him but betrayed him with his own brother. Nate had his own landscaping business and kept his own hours and had always combed his hair and cleaned up before coming for dinner at Chuck and Sharmela's. Sharmela, who had the whole summer off from teaching while Chuck was working at least sixty hours a week at the bakery he'd opened six months ago. Business was booming, all right. He sighed.

"Hey, Gus!" he shouted, not looking back. He could see the three of them in front of another large rock formation that looked like a big pile of shit. Merlene was standing between Gus and Vernon, physically keeping them apart. They paid no attention to Chuck as he jostled up beside them.

"You can get *lost* in these caves, you know, big shot!" Gus shouted at Vernon. "You need *me* to find the way out."

"Lincoln's fucking ghost. This kid's too much. Let me at him!" Vernon shouted back, leaning into Merlene. Chuck shuddered as Sharmela touched his elbow, rejoining the group.

"Stop it. Somebody could fall over the edge. It looks pretty far down there," Sharmela said. Everybody looked at her. People always looked at Sharmela. She had this easy authority that comes from teaching elementary school. And she was beautiful, her long black hair and lean figure suggesting that she would always be beautiful, even in old age. She had poise and grace. Chuck expected her to tell them to put their heads on their desks for five minutes, or to stay after school, or apologize to each other. It was a deep drop over the railing. They all backed away from the edge, even Gus. Merlene let out an exaggerated "Whew."

"Let's just get out of here," Chuck said. "I think we've all seen enough. Hey, Gus, is there something about the air in here that makes people nuts? I suppose I'm asking the wrong guy. Everybody seems a little crazy."

"What are you talking about, Chuck?" Sharmela asked. It was like he'd given the wrong answer in class. Chuck didn't want to stay after school for what was probably the final lesson.

"Even me?" Merlene said, half-flirtatiously. Vernon snorted.

"No, not you, Marlene. Maybe we should run off together and leave these saps behind," Chuck said.

"It's *Mer*lene," Vernon corrected.

"He just got forced into retirement at Little's Shoes," Merlene explained, "and he's not too happy about it."

"Oh, sure, just go and tell everybody!" Vernon shouted. "Let the whole world know. Hey, everybody, Vernon Little got put out to pasture!"

"It's just the three of us, not the whole world," Gus said, remarkably calm for such a young, pimply-faced geek. "I'm sorry you lost your job. Just don't make me lose mine, okay?"

"Hey, if it's Little's Shoes, and you're Little, how can anybody force you out?" Chuck asked. "I got my own bakery, and nobody can make me quit."

"Just because," Vernon said.

"You're young, son," Merlene said. "But someday you'll be old."

"Wow, heavy," Chuck said, and even he wasn't sure if he was mocking her or not.

Gus shrugged. "And now," he said, moving forward again, "we move to the light show part of the tour."

Sharmela was quiet and grim. Whatever she was going to say would have to wait. Though she'd practically said it already—it was just the details that she needed to fill in. And if it *was* Nate, Chuck knew he'd need a lot of details.

■　■　■

Last time we left our heroes, they were stranded in the Cave of Death with the evil Doctor Truth.

Vernon played the drums in the high school band. He was the Wild Drummer. Then he sold shoes. The Wild Shoe Salesman. Now he was the Wild Retiree. His friends called him Vern for short, but he didn't have many of those. C'mon, Vern, old pal, old buddy, don't be moping when you could be groping, don't be frowning when you could be clowning. Vernon wore his beeper in the cave, but it was only a prop now. If he only had some accomplices on the outside.

Gus. Get on the bus, Gus. Stuck in a cave all summer while his buddies guided fishing or canoeing trips on the Muskegon River. His buddies picking up babes left and right, from what he hears—though Gus doesn't hear much hundreds of feet beneath the earth. His friends rescuing damsels from the clutches of, yes, they had named a rapid Devil's Staircase, too—the devil must've built a lot of staircases. The devil is in the details. If only he'd learned to swim, damn it. The more his father insisted that it was the one thing he had no choice about, the more he'd resisted. He had a constant cold down under, his skin an unhealthy grayish white. He was trying to grow a beard with little success.

And then we've got Sharm the Charm. She's ready to dump Chuck and move on to brother Nate. Inconvenient, yes. To become more inconvenient, yes again. Hey, at least she wasn't a nun. Hey, at least they'd lasted ten years. Hey, even the scrawny guide Gus was starting to look good. So, a little experimental romp in the hay with her brother-in-law had become, what? No guilt, so that's a sign, ain't it? That's what they said at Crossroads. Damn it, Chuck so boring, nothing about him to even piss her off. Just annoy her.

Well, divorcing him should get him going. Get him going and keep Sharm coming. She laughed to herself. Internal monologues, her latest bad habit. She might even start smoking.

And in this corner, Merlene, suddenly stuck with Mr. Little and his sad story. She was a mother "from the old school." Finally free of that, but now she had this new child interrupting her days, adjusting the air conditioner and complaining about her knickknacks. Too late now, buster. She's keeping a clipboard and chart, trying to get him out exploring the world, or at least western Michigan. Here they are in a cave, and he's trying to pick a fight. She'll have to spank *him* when they get home.

And Chuck in a neutral corner. Mr. Neutral, Mr. Idle, Mr. Whatever-you-say. Bowing down to the Great Whoever. Bowing down to all corners of the earth, not taking any chances. Making communion wafers for the world. Matzoth. Whatever. Why didn't the Big It make staircases? There was "Stairway to Heaven." . . . Well, we know enough about Chuck, I think.

All we need now is a cave-in. Or a murder. Or a commercial break. Helloooooo down there, spelunkers!

■　■　■

Last time we left our heroes. . . . The lights whizzed and whirled around the cave. This was the part Gus still loved, even after weeks on the job. Though he wanted to replace the Led Zeppelin soundtrack with something more contemporary—some White Lies or Raging Panic. Man, *that'd* get the stalactites shaking. The other guide was the owner's grandson. *Mikey,* Gus sneered disdainfully. Mikey, whom Gus called the Mole because he enjoyed the cave so much. He'd grown up down there and had explored every inch of it, knew how far every passage went. He was part of a cave rescue unit that traveled around to all the caves in Indiana, Ohio, Pennsylvania, Kentucky, rescuing people. He was, in short, a mole. And Gus, in short, was not.

Chuck knew this was his story, and he would have to get control of it. If only they could get out of the cave. Sharmela liked the dark a little too much, he thought.

"Wow," he said, and put his arms around her waist as they watched the rock formations sparkle and glow around them, dancing to the music. He wasn't planning on letting go.

It wasn't as much fun smoking alone, but Chuck wasn't going to give it up. He was growing it himself now, in the closet with lights. "I should have done this years ago," he told Sharmela. "Frankly," she said, "prayer is more interesting." She thought it was weird, him sitting in the living room getting high by himself.

Sharm got in trouble in the nunnery for making up her own prayers. Her role model was Saint Teresa. "Man, that chick had the spirit," she said. They told her she didn't have what it takes after she shunned Sister Satan. Sharmela said she *did* have what it takes, and that was the problem.

"Wow, indeed," she replied. She peeled Chuck's hands off her. She had to take care of business while they were still safe underground.

"Beeeautiful!" Vern shouted, to make sure everyone could hear him above the music.

"Yeah!" Chuck yelled, the sound echoing back to him, giving him a brief moment of satisfaction.

Merlene felt like an astronaut exploring the surface of a distant planet. She wanted to go for a space walk, but she couldn't loosen her tight grip on the slimy railing beneath her hand. Her hand landed on top of Sharmela's, and they drew back from each other in the rhythmic dark and light of that artificial storm. All hands on deck. Every man for himself. Every woman for herself.

Gus scrapped the whole narration and just let them watch. He wondered if he could get a job at the Detroit Science Center with his experience here. Get into the city, away from those hick river guides. You don't have to swim in college, he thought, and that's where *he* was going.

The light and sound show ended suddenly, and the entire cave fell into dark silence. Gus liked the little panic this inspired—he could feel it in the air after all the loose talking. For this particular group, he lengthened the pause before flicking the switch on the floodlights.

■　■　■

"So, you have now seen the one natural cave in the whole state of Michigan."

"One too many," Chuck mumbled.

"Any questions?" Gus asked wearily, hoping they'd all take the hint.

"Isn't it creepy being down here all day?" Merlene asked.

"What do you mean?" He was squinting at his watch. It might have stopped.

"It's kind of like you're buried. I can't help thinking that if we never got out of the cave, how many people would care? How long would it take them to notice? I'm seventy-three years old, and there's not a half-dozen people who'd do more than blink if they never saw me again."

"That's heavy shit," Sharmela said. "See, that's why I have to split up with Chuck."

Why couldn't rocks just be rocks? Why couldn't a flat tire be a flat tire? Chuck didn't like the idea of breaking up underground with witnesses. It wasn't like breaking up in high school when you got drunk and then got a new girlfriend the next day. How was he going to bake all that bread through his grief?

"Not that again," Vernon said. "That's not true, dear," he said, turning to Merlene. "You would be missed by many."

"*I'd* miss you," Chuck said, trying to change the channel.

"But you're down here with me, so you couldn't miss me."

They seemed to have forgotten about Gus and how he felt about working underground. How he felt was pretty lousy. Permanently cold. After work, squinting in the bright natural light. He thought he was going blind. He couldn't see underground *or* aboveground.

Vernon had just listed about twenty people who he insisted would be devastated by Merlene's demise.

"Remember me?" Chuck said. "Your husband?" This was hell. The Big It wasn't into fire like everyone thought. He was into the cold and the dark. And shame and embarrassment and panic and terror, all of which Chuck felt at that moment as he prepared himself to go up Devil's Staircase and out into Devil's World, where he'd get into Devil's Car with the unflat tire and drive home in the Devil's Silence with his soon-to-be-ex-wife who believed in nothing except the underground and the art and science of landscaping. And Crossroads allowed no hesitation, believing that change was good, always good.

Sharmela suddenly took off her gold band and diamond engagement ring, and tried to hand them both to Chuck. He pulled his hand back, and the rings clinked off rocks and disappeared into a crevice.

Gus turned back. "Somebody drop something?"

"Just some pennies!" Chuck shouted, intent on blindness. "For luck!"

"Devil's pennies," Vernon said.

"Devil's irony," Merlene said. "Make a wish."

"Oops," Sharmela said.

Then, to the surprise of everyone, the Great Whoever flicked off the lights again, just as they were ready to ascend. It's not often you can find such pure darkness. They could all hear each other breathing. Briefly, they all could have been anyone, anywhere, and briefly they were.

Short Season

"I'll trade you my five-year plan for your ten-year plan," Debi said.
Her son, Albert, was clattering down the stairs in his new soccer
cleats, ready for practice. I was the coach. Coach K. My daughter,
Carol, was waiting in the van outside in her enormous gold T-shirt
with the number 9 on the back—9, her age.

"I don't have a ten-year plan," I said truthfully. "Or a five-year
plan—whoa, I just got this very intense déjà vu when I said that.
Weird."

"What, did some other dying friend come on to you in a previous life?" Debi asked, getting up slowly, adjusting her wig.

"I had no previous life," I said. Then Albert was on top of us,
scrabbling over the tile floor, slamming into me.

"Don't those cleats have brakes on them?" I asked.

"They don't come with brakes," Albert said enthusiastically.
Albert was definitely an Albert. I was relatively confident no one
would ever call him Al. He was tall, gangly, and effeminate. He
liked playing make-believe with my daughter when he came over

for play dates, and I'd invariably find them both in dresses down in the basement.

I was divorced from Alicia, my second wife. Carol was my only child. Rachel, my first wife, had fled before the notion of having children had even been a tiny gnat in the swamp of her brain. Alicia, on the other hand, left me with Carol to pursue a lesbian relationship. She and her partner, Rita, had Carol on weekends. Part of the problem was that I still loved Alicia. I hadn't had sex with anyone since she'd bailed on me a year and a half ago. And then I got propositioned by Debi, who was dying of breast cancer—it had spread through her body, a crazed hit man spraying lethal bullets at all her organs, and here she was bald and without breasts and staring at me with what looked nothing and everything like lust.

"C'mon, Sparky," I said. "Go climb in the van with Carol, and I'll be right there." Albert skidded out the door, and I heard the van door sliding open and the two kids giggling.

"It's not like they can just let me die—they have to turn me into some kind of freak first," she said, falling into my arms. "I wish I had cleats that wouldn't let me stop. Kevin, I just want to crash into everybody."

The bubbles of the soap opera of my own life were popping in the air above us. "I'm still thinking about that déjà vu," I said.

"Oh, Kevin," she said. "You don't have to fuck me. I just wish Toby would."

"I wish Alicia would still fuck me. She could bring Rita along, for all I care." Toby was her husband, a big-league attorney who had no time for soccer or sex.

"You are an asshole. I take it all back."

"How is Toby dealing with things these days?" I knew he was a human pit of despair, no help to anyone, but it seemed like asking was the right thing to do, considering the proposition on the table, floating around us like fall turning to winter. Would it be her last winter? The answer was yes. Not that I could've handled it any better than Toby.

I hadn't seen him since Debi had started chemo, and the word had spread through school like hair falling out in chunks, everybody acknowledging it, nobody sweeping it up. Since Alicia had left me, I had found myself in the curious company of the other mothers at school meetings, on field trips, and in the daily dropoff/pickup our lives seemed to revolve around.

I was a teacher myself, at Dondero High, the closest public school to Digby, the private school our kids attended. My schedule allowed me to participate actively in Carol's school activities, which made me a hero of sorts among some of the other mothers. Though others kept their distance—suspicious, I think, of any man who'd drive his wife into the arms of another woman. And suspicious of cancer, for a curious hushed border surrounded Debi in her brief public appearances at the school, when she was feeling up to it.

"Dad, c'mon, we're gonna be late!" Carol shouted.

"Dad, c'mon, we're gonna be late!" Albert echoed.

"What does that tell you about Toby?" Debi asked.

"We're gonna be late?" I replied, grasping for the handle on the screen door. Toby hadn't put the storms in, or had somebody do it, though it was late October, and the chill filtered through.

Debi turned and walked away from me without another word.

■　■　■

I willingly take on the role of an unsympathetic character here. The one who lives on. Just as I took on the role of the "good" parent without comment or protestation. My old friend Jeff from college got a dog and used it to lure girls to the house we shared with two other art majors, while the truth was, he neglected that dog, leaving it unfed, unwalked, letting it unhappily pace across the cold linoleum till it began chewing up the corners of paintings and album covers and stray socks and a shoe or two. Shortly before graduation, Jeff took the dog out into the country, let it out of his pickup, and drove off. He said it ran away, but years later, over a bottle of vodka, he'd admitted the truth. He'd thought it was better than taking it to the pound. Hmm. What do you think? The dog's name was Buddha.

We're all frauds in one way or another. It's a matter of determining which frauds are more forgivable. Excusable. Perhaps endearing.

Debi and I knew each other from way back—pre-Toby, who'd moved to Detroit to attend Wayne State's law school. We'd attended grade school together at Saint Vincent's, then high school at Bishop Murphy. We'd had one date, in eleventh grade. I took her to midnight mass on Christmas Eve, then we made out in her driveway, Christmas lights blurring in through the steamy windows. Then four of our classmates died in a drunk driving accident on New Year's Eve. The newspapers were all over it. We were there together, one funeral after another. Then we went back to school, and back to just being friends.

Our families were close, so it might have been hard to go very far with it, anyway. We might have ended up feeling like we were kissing our cousins or something like that. Though when my brother, Phil, moved to Atlanta, where our cousin Janet lived, he dated her long enough to investigate what states allowed you to marry your cousin. Apparently, there are a few. The family never knew. Phil's my twin and still tells me nearly everything.

■　■　■

"Guess what?"

Phil and I never identified ourselves or even said hello on the phone. It was always as if we were just picking up from a pause in one long conversation.

"You finally won a soccer game?"

"Nah, that's never gonna happen. It's bad news. Debi Reed's dying of cancer."

"Shit." Phil had dated Debi when they were both at Michigan State. Our Royal Oak neighborhood was a small town, the lives intersecting a thousand odd ways. Phil and I had dated a number of the same women.

We sat breathing at each other till I finally said, "Yeah . . . she's in bad shape. That Toby guy is apparently being a bastard about it. She kind of came on to me the other day when I was picking up her kid for soccer."

"Shit," Phil said again. He was still living in Atlanta, still single. I sometimes joke that I got married twice, once for me, once for Phil. Though if I ever get married again, I don't know what I'll say. Cousin Janet moved to California years ago and married a dentist from Croatia.

"How does a dying person come on to you?" he asked, though I don't think he wanted an answer. At least, I didn't give him one.

■ ■ ■

Did you ever have one of those days where you just looked out the window all the time, thinking someone was going to drop in? Kept imagining you heard the phone ringing or a knock on the door? On weekends, when Carol was staying with Alicia, I'd be afraid to play my music too loud for fear of not hearing something, some faint wisp of human contact.

■ ■ ■

How can you say yes? How can you say no?

She died two months later. It's no fun going there, so I won't.

■ ■ ■

"Fucking won't solve anything."

"Fucking won't keep you from dying."

"Fucking's just another word for nothin' left to lose."

"Fucking is to dying as eating is to shitting."

"Fucking is the world's invisible report card."

Phil said some of those things. I didn't list them all. I didn't list all the silence.

■　■　■

As the coach of the Pee-Wee Maroons (the league did not allow names, only colors; at least it wasn't Birch, a name that just confused everybody), I saw Debi many times as her clock slowed its ticking, muted it so that every noise in that house seemed to be an erasure. Till her mother moved in to help, and Debi and I were forced into brief, hushed conversations as if we were dating teenagers under her mother's watchful eye. Till they moved her to a hospice and she disappeared.

"Why did your mom name you Debi like that, only one b and an i instead of a y?" I knew her middle name, her saint's name, was Agnes. Debi Agnes Reed. "You always seemed like two b's and a y to me."

We could not talk about her condition anymore. We both knew it was only worse and more worse. It was all we could do not to discuss her in the past tense. When I picked up Albert, I was torn, knowing both that she was back there somewhere in her dark room and that I did not, not really, want to see her. All Albert could do was push through his routines in numb wonder. During the games, he would drift off, away from the action, staring at some speck on the ground, some invisible marking on his hand that had perhaps caused all this.

"Go Maroon!" I shouted, all I was allowed to say under the strict league guidelines for coaches. My daughter, Carol, touched Albert in a way and with a frequency I would consider unnatural under different circumstances, constantly hugging him, sitting on his lap, playing with his hair. My theory was that she felt if she touched him enough, he wouldn't fade away like his mother was doing. I didn't want to bring it up—and say, say what? "Don't touch your friend, his mother's dying, and you might catch it"?

Her touching him made me all the more conflicted about not having sex with Debi. I'd like to go back and ask old Sister Cyril, our sixth-grade teacher, about that one. Would that be a sin? For both of us? Where would God come down on that one?

■ ■ ■

"I told Phil," I said. It was a bad day, and she was plastered to her bed while Albert searched for his shin guards.

"Yeah," she said. "Good old Phil. I could always tell."

"What? Can I get you something?" Her mother was out doing the shopping.

"Tell the difference. Between you two."

"I'm the better kisser, right?" I was bringing it up myself, the idea of sex. It created a new tension in the room to distract her. The potential for something else happening besides dying. Or maybe I did it to distract myself.

"Yeah, right," she said, and closed her eyes. I went to help Albert get ready. We were running late again, as usual. They couldn't start without me, I always said.

■ ■ ■

Debi had always been wiry or frail, depending on the quality of light and what she'd done the night before. Night had always energized her. She had been a cheerleader for night, urging it on, wanting it never to end. In high school, she was at every party, screaming her greetings at each new arrival, her every gesture or remark magnified by darkness. She herself was a magnifier, for she liked to drink. She could hold her liquor. None of us knew where it went, but not to her head. At parties, she was the alluring light that drew the bugs, the thugs. That drew guys like Phil and me.

Before she became ill, when we waited outside school for the children to be released to our care, Debi had often reflected on how we'd ended up with respectable lives. Debi didn't age like the rest of us, falling into our late thirties with bad backs, big bellies, butts, anxieties. From the back, she could still be mistaken for a teenage girl, and I think before the cancer she had still imagined herself as sixteen, bouncing with energy and enthusiasm for the smallest little triumph of Albert's young life. She saw her marriage to Toby as an impulsive aberration rather that a logical step toward maturity. We all thought it wouldn't last, and maybe it wouldn't have. The cancer was aging her a year for every day she lived with it.

■ ■ ■

"You don't know anything about soccer. What are you doing coaching?" She had poured me a cup of coffee when I dropped Albert off after a game one Sunday. Her illness had recently been diagnosed. Toby came out into the kitchen, said hello, and went back to his game—whatever football game happened to be on TV that afternoon. The kids often wanted to continue playing together, so we'd given them a half-hour before I took Carol back to Alicia's for the rest of the afternoon.

"You kick a ball in a net. All I have to do is point them in the right direction," I said. "And shout, 'Go Maroon!'"

"But why?" she persisted. I didn't really need the coffee, but it stole me a little more time out of my weekend alone. "You're free to date on weekends," Alicia had said on numerous occasions, "and you get to skip half the birthday parties we have to drag her to." It was like she was pressuring me to date, to have a new "partner" to balance things out in the odd equation of our child's life.

"Okay, how about this." With Debi, I tended not to bullshit around. Perhaps she knew me too well—I always felt I had to come clean with her. "It's because I think soccer's the one sport I could've been good at if we'd had it when we were growing up." I was short, thin, and strategic. The holy trinity of football, basketball, and baseball dominated our school. Soccer was viewed suspiciously as a foreign game—and you couldn't use your hands. It's true that while on the sideline shouting "Go Maroon!" and pointing in the direction they were to go, I sometimes imagined what I could've done in a game like soccer. A game played all over the world. All you needed was a ball.

"You were good at lots of sports—kickball in the street . . ."

"Aha!" I interrupted. "See, *kick*ball. Kicking. I could always kick, remember?"

My favorite thing was the concept of ghost runners—you left invisible runners on base when it was your turn to be up again in the odd three-on-three games we used to play in the street. You could drive in your own ghost with a timely hit.

We both took great joy in remembering the minutiae of our childhoods. Perhaps Toby was right to ignore us and watch the game, the game happening *now*.

"Okay, it gives me some structure so I'm not sitting home feeling sorry for myself. Though I know I don't have anything to feel sorry about," I added quickly.

■ ■ ■

I should probably come clean now. I've been holding out so I wouldn't sound so sappy. Debi was the first girl I ever kissed, and yes, I wrote her name in my notebook and made the dot of the i into a heart. Seventh grade, in the dark space between the brick walls of two houses on our tightly packed street. We kissed so long and so hard my lips hurt the next day.

When you saw somebody every day like I saw Debi back then, the idea of a continued romantic involvement seemed completely absurd and plausible. If I would have been able to carry an empty pop bottle around and spin it whenever I ran into Debi, perhaps we would have been able to keep something going, but without my props I was hopeless and fell back on kickball in the street and on tormenting Crazy Eddie, the neighborhood grouch. Who also died of cancer, the Pall Malls doing him in. That, and the meanness, we'd thought back then. Now we knew meanness had nothing to do with it. Debi never smoked.

When you see somebody dying whom you have known forever, the idea of even a brief romantic involvement seems completely absurd and plausible.

■ ■ ■

"Okay, I'll sleep with you, and that'll turn you into a lesbian, and that'll at least make the rest of your life more interesting," I said.

"How many women have you played that lesbian card on?"

"Just a few. I don't meet many women."

"But you use it every time you do."

"Yeah, well, practically—it gets right to the point that the conversation's going to end up at, anyway: Married? Divorced. What happened? My wife left me for another woman. At least this way, I can get a laugh out of it. They seem a little curious. It disarms them."

"This dying thing, Kevin, it's a drag. A total and complete bummer." She sighed as if blowing out the smoke from a hit on a joint—exaggerated like that. Was she playing the dying card on me?

"Toby, he'll make sure I have everything I need. Material things. 'The best doctors,' he keeps saying. He knows all the best doctors, you know. No, it's true. All that malpractice work."

I laughed.

"That came out wrong, I suppose." She grabbed my fingers and stretched and pulled at them. "Just hold my fucking hand, will you? But every time I want to talk, he gets completely freaked out. It's like when I tried to tell Albert about sex and he covered his ears and ran out of the room screaming."

"I can't picture Albert screaming."

"He screamed."

I squeezed her hand, and we made one big lumpy fist. *Lump,* a word that forever would be one heavy stone to sink to the bottom of every murky lake, to crash through every clear perfect window.

"Kevin, I don't want to fuck you. I just want to *talk about* fucking you. I mean, what would we do? I want to imagine it. Imagine it back when we were kids, but we know what we know now." She looked out into the yard at our two kids making mysterious stews out of various weeds and sticks.

"That's good. I'm glad you added that last part. Otherwise, I would've come before I even got inside you."

"That's your choice, we talk about fucking or dying today, old friend," she said so firmly that I knew I wasn't going to just slip out the door into the sunshine and hold my daughter's hand and drive off like I so suddenly and desperately wanted to.

"How far should we go?" I asked. I'm the bad guy, remember.

"All the way, baby, all the way," she replied in a mock throaty whisper that ended in a coughing fit. "Okay," she said when she was through. "Forget that coughing part—that probably wasn't much of a turn-on. Let's start *now.*"

■ ■ ■

I'm going to stop now. I don't think I can do it—to bring back our conversation at her kitchen table in the stiff wooden chairs without sounding like some lurid advertisement for phone sex or something. It was nothing like that, how we tenderly interrupted each other and steered each other's words down an impossibly soft, smooth path, and to the gentlest of landings. It was like watching our ghost runners, driving them home. Afterward, we sat silently together in the dusk that was not only gathering but accumulating permanently.

Then I called Carol in. Soon I would have to tell her that her best friend's mother was not just sick but dying for real and forever. Carol was muddy and disheveled and excited. She wanted to show us their secret potions before we left. Debi and I dutifully rose, and I led her into the yard to look at their dark, wet concoctions that could cure everything and nothing.

Carol and Albert smiled expectantly up at us. "Good," we said together, then "Great," I said when I saw that was what was called for. "Yeah, great," Debi repeated. "Great," we said together again.